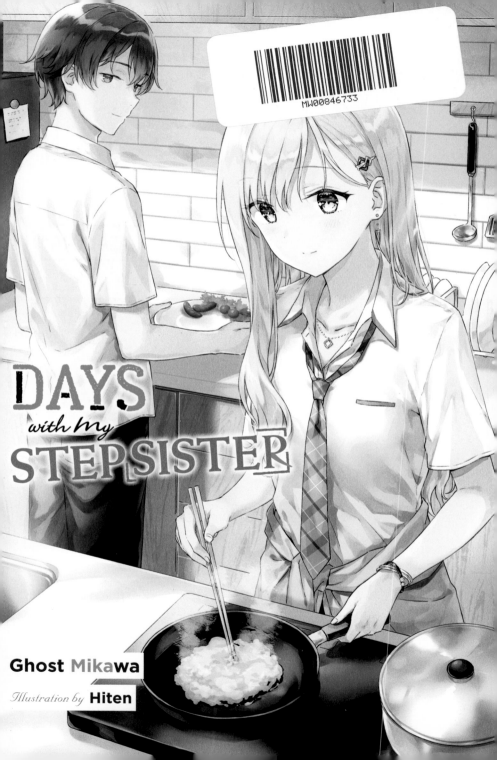

DAYS
*with My*
STEPSISTER

**Ghost Mikawa**

*Illustration by* **Hiten**

SAKI AYASE

Hmm. So Asamura wanted to watch this show, too. That's great, since I was also interested in checking it out.

MY STEPSISTER
DURING PE

MY STEPSISTER
AT NIGHT

# DAYS
*with My*
# STEP SISTER

# 1

**Ghost Mikawa**

*Illustration by* **Hiten**

YEN
ON

New York

# DAYS *with* *my* STEPSISTER 1

## Ghost Mikawa

Translation by Eriko Sugita ● Cover art by Hiten

GIMAISEIKATSU Vol. 1
©Ghost Mikawa 2021
First published in Japan in 2021 by KADOKAWA CORPORATION, Tokyo.
English translation rights arranged with KADOKAWA CORPORATION, Tokyo
through TUTTLE-MORI AGENCY, INC., Tokyo.

English translation © 2023 by Yen Press, LLC

Yen On
150 West 30th Street, 19th Floor, New York, NY 10001

Visit us at yenpress.com • facebook.com/yenpress • twitter.com/yenpress
yenpress.tumblr.com • instagram.com/yenpress

First Yen On Edition: October 2023
Edited by Yen On Editorial: Emma McClain
Designed by Yen Press Design: Wendy Chan

Library of Congress Cataloging-in-Publication Data
Names: Mikawa, Ghost, author. | Hiten (Illustrator), illustrator. |
Sugita, Eriko. translation.
Title: Days with my stepsister / Ghost Mikawa ; illustration by Hiten ;
translation by Eriko Sugita.
Other titles: Gimai seikatsu. English
Description: First Yen On edition. | New York, NY : Yen On, 2023–
Identifiers: LCCN 2023024502 | ISBN 9781975372033 (v. 1 ; trade paperback)
Subjects: CYAC: Stepbrothers—Fiction. | Stepsisters—Fiction. | Love—Fiction. |
LCGFT: Romance fiction. | Light novels.
Classification: LCC PZ7.1.M5537 Day 2023 | DDC [Fic]—dc23
LC record available at https://lccn.loc.gov/2023024502

ISBNs: 978-1-9753-7203-3 (paperback)
978-1-9753-7204-0 (ebook)

10 9 8 7 6 5 4 3 2 1

LSC-C

Printed in the United States of America

# DAYS
## *with My*
# STEPSISTER

## Saki Ayase

A high school junior who becomes Yuuta's stepsister after their parents remarry. Her flashy outfits tend to make people think she is a bad girl, and she has a hard time blending in at school.

"Things would be easy if the whole of humanity could just be chill, like you and me."

"You might repay me one day, so it's a win-win."

"Whoa! You must be the big brother Saki's been telling me about! So it *is* you— Yuuta Asamura from the next class over!"

## Maaya Narasaka

Saki's classmate. She's always full of energy and loves to meddle. Unable to bear seeing Saki isolated in class, she cheerfully forced her way into becoming Saki's friend.

## Yuuta Asamura

A high school junior. He becomes Saki's older stepbrother after his dad marries Saki's mom. He's an average high schooler, but he distances himself from others. He loves to read and is addicted to books.

## Taichi Asamura

**"I've decided to get married."**

Yuuta's dad and Saki's stepfather. A lot happened with his first wife, whom he divorced before eventually marrying Akiko Ayase. Taichi gets along well with Yuuta and Saki.

## Tomokazu Maru

Yuuta's classmate and probably his only friend at school. He's on the baseball team and is a huge nerd.

**"So I hear you have a sister now, huh? You're a big brother, you lucky dog."**

**"I appreciate it. You're a really dependable guy, Yuuta."**

**"Tee-hee. Taichi told me all about you. My, you look put together."**

## Shiori Yomiuri

Shiori is a college student who works part-time at a bookstore with Yuuta. She's rooting for him in his relationship with his stepsister.

## Akiko Ayase

Saki's mom and Yuuta's stepmother. After divorcing her ex-husband, she devoted herself to her work and raised Saki single-handedly until her second marriage.

# Contents

Days with My Stepsister

Frontispiece and illustrations by Hiten

This is a story about this girl and me—two strangers until yesterday— and how we became *family*…

# ● PROLOGUE

I can say this because I've experienced it—a stepsister is nothing more than a stranger.

Arriving at that truth in my second year of high school was a huge bummer for me as an adolescent guy, but it was really lucky considering my family situation. In manga, light novels, and games, the lack of blood ties between stepsiblings becomes an excuse for romance, and after some twists and turns, they always end up together. It would have been so cringey if I'd taken all that seriously and gotten my hopes up. I probably would've wound up playing the protective older brother like some cliché protagonist or something.

But reality isn't like that.

So you're probably wondering, how is a real-life stepsister different from the kind guys fantasize about? Well, let me give you an example. I get home from my part-time job at the bookstore and see my stepsister sitting on the couch drinking hot cocoa. This is how our conversation goes:

"Hi, Asamura."

"Hi, Ayase."

That's it.

Get it?

She's not going to say, "Hey there, older brother ♪," in a sweet, syrupy tone. She won't say something openly hostile like, "Ugh. You stink. Don't talk to me, stepbrother," either. You're cool, you're strangers—you simply exchange plain old matter-of-fact greetings.

She's not going to act cutesy and fawn on you, nor will she hurl abuse at you. Both of those ideas are equally out of touch with reality.

Of course, there's no heart-fluttering, lovey-dovey stuff, excessive respect, or codependence between my stepsister and me. We've existed in this world for sixteen years, and our paths never crossed. You can't tell us we'll be family starting the next day and expect us to suddenly have special feelings for each other.

I'd have more intense feelings about someone who wound up in the same class as me two years in a row.

My name is Yuuta Asamura. I'll be turning sixteen this year, and I'm in my second year of high school.

If you're wondering how I ended up with a new stepsister at my age, it's because my dad is *energetic*. I respect him from the bottom of my heart for deciding to marry again after what he went through.

As far back as I can remember, my parents were always fighting, and I wasn't surprised when Dad told me they were getting divorced. He apologized and said it was because he was a worthless man, but I knew it was because Mom had an affair, and I listened to him with no illusions.

After that, I lived my life without expecting much from the women of our species. That is, until one afternoon, when Dad made a sudden announcement. I was pulling out the key for my bicycle lock and sticking a foot in my sneaker at the door when he said it.

"I've decided to get married."

"Huh?"

"You don't mind, do you? She's a beautiful lady with a big heart."

"I don't know. Adjectives alone don't tell me what type of person she is."

"Her three sizes from the top are thirty-six, twenty-four, and thirty-five."

"Numbers aren't any better, you know...and do you really think that's the first info a son wants about his new mom?"

"Aren't you happy that she has a fantastic figure?"

"Not particularly."

"What...?! Can a teenage boy really be so unmoved by sexual desire? I always thought you seemed a little cold, but wow..."

"Hey."

I clapped back at my dad, telling him that was a rude way to think of his own son.

People often get the wrong idea when I say I don't expect much from women. All I'm saying is that I don't count on receiving any warmth and kindness from them. I still get excited when I see a naked woman and horny when I see girls wearing bathing suits during swimming class.

That said, I'm not so undisciplined that I would start lusting over my dad's girlfriend—someone who might become my mother.

"That aside, Dad, I'm amazed to hear that you've met someone at forty. Does she work at your office?"

"She was working at a bar my boss brought me to. She took care of me when I got wasted after drinking too much."

"Are you sure she isn't tricking you into marrying her...?"

I didn't necessarily subscribe to cliché ideas like "people working in bars and clubs are all criminals and con artists," but because of Dad's bad experience in the past, it was easy to see the negative.

"Of course not. Akiko, at least, isn't like that. Ah-ha-ha-ha!"

Dad roared with laughter. But wasn't that exactly what someone being tricked would say? I was frankly appalled.

Still, I didn't fight him on it.

"Whatever makes you happy is fine with me," I said. "I'll just live the same way I've always lived."

That was what I meant by not getting my hopes up. Because I had no expectations about this new life with a new mom, I wasn't worried about any potential negatives, either—like if we ended up being unhappy or she was fooling my dad into marrying her. At the time, I was just thinking I'd let whatever happened happen.

"I don't think that'll be so easy," Dad replied. "You'll have a younger sister, after all."

"Huh? A younger sister?"

"That's right. Akiko's daughter. She showed me a picture. The girl was pretty cute."

So this woman, Akiko, was divorced like Dad. It sounded like they had both experienced a failed marriage, and I bet having that in common helped bring them together.

"See? Isn't she cute?"

"Oh...um, yeah."

Dad seemed really excited as he lifted his phone to show me a picture of a little girl, probably in the first few years of elementary school. A foreign fantasy novel translated into Japanese and aimed at young children was spread across her lap. She was staring shyly into the camera.

"Congratulations," he said. "You're now a big brother!"

"Don't try to win me over with a grin and a thumbs-up... Well, she *is* a cute kid. I guess I wouldn't mind having her around."

A teenage little sister sounded like a hassle, but if she was an elementary schooler, that was different. For your information, I'm not into little girls or anything. I thought she was cute, but not like that. Just regular cute, okay? Anyway, I was relieved that she was almost ten years younger than me because it meant I wouldn't have to walk on eggshells around her.

"We're getting together around nine tonight," said my dad, "so when you get off work, drop by Royal Host. You know, the restaurant near the bookstore."

"Isn't this a little sudden...?"

"Ha-ha. I meant to tell you, and then a whole month went by in a flash. I guess I kind of let it slip until the day of."

"A whole month?!"

"Ha-ha. Sorry about that."

That's my dad for you. I watched him scratch his temple, smiling sheepishly, and sighed. He might seem unreliable, but you could tell he was a good man underneath.

"Okay, I'll be there," I said. "Be grateful I'm not a delinquent who takes off in the middle of the night."

"I've never been worried about something like that. I trust you."

He really was a good guy, my dad.

A new mom. A new sister. A new family.

Letting those words drift around unsettled in my head, I somehow managed to finish my shift, though my senior colleague (a real babe) said she thought I was phoning it in.

As Devora Zack says, it's the height of stupidity to multitask, and focusing on one thing at a time increases efficiency. I told my colleague that I believed concentrating on having a successful first meeting with my grade-school-age stepsister-to-be was more important, and that was why I was only going through the motions at work. She was not impressed.

I thought she was being unreasonable, since she was the one who told me about Zack's book in the first place. But when I finished my shift and headed out, she slapped my back and said, "Go for it, Big Brother!" I always knew she was a good person deep down.

It was nighttime in Shibuya. I rode my bicycle from the bookstore where I worked up Dogenzaka Hill for a few minutes and arrived at the restaurant Dad had specified. It was a busy time of day, and the doorway was packed with groups of young women. I overheard them complaining about their boyfriends.

A woman with a deep tan and an avant-garde updo, wearing a flashy outfit, was saying her guy had bad taste in clothes and little experience with women, and he couldn't understand a girl's heart.

I felt like saying to her, "Uh, excuse me, are you sure you want to be making fun of someone else when you're dressed like *that*? Maybe you should complain directly to your boyfriend if you aren't happy with him."

But of course, I could never say that, so I passed them by and started looking for my dad, who had already arrived. He'd texted me directions to where he was sitting, and I tried to follow them.

I hoped I never had to deal with flashy women like that who expected way too much from men. I was so glad the stepsister I was about to meet was a grade-schooler—though again, I'm not into that kind of thing. I didn't get my hopes up, but I quietly prayed that she wouldn't grow up to be like those women by the door.

"Hey, Yuuta. Over here."

Dad must have noticed me looking around. He was seated by a window, waving to me.

I looked down, embarrassed that the other patrons were staring at us, and promptly went to his table.

I could already feel a seed of discomfort budding in my mind.

It got bigger with every step I took, planted its roots firmly, and sprouted when I saw our new family members sitting across from Dad. A flower of confusion bloomed when I reached his table.

Something wasn't right. What was going on here?

"Hello! You must be Yuuta. I'm sorry we had you come out here right after work."

"N-not at all. I'm Yuuta Asamura. You must be…"

"Akiko Ayase. Tee-hee. Taichi told me all about you. My, you look put together."

I was standing there, completely bewildered. The woman who first spoke to me—the one who introduced herself as Akiko Ayase—smiled happily as she said my dad's name with a touch of familiarity.

She had something of a baby face, but her gaze and expressions gave off a mature kind of sex appeal. Dad hadn't been exaggerating when he'd described her as a beautiful lady with a big heart. She made me think of a dandelion that grew in the city at night.

But this gorgeous woman wasn't what was confusing me.

It was the person sitting next to her who caught my attention—my eyes were glued to her. I recognized her face from the photo. This must be the girl who was about to become my stepsister. But she was nothing like I had expected.

"Come on, say hello!" her mother said to her.

"Okay," she replied.

The girl straightened her back until she looked like a well-carved statuette. Then she ran her fingers through her brightly dyed hair as the earrings in her pierced ears sparkled a dull silver, and she shot me a mysterious smile.

"Hi. I'm Saki Ayase."

"Oh, um, hi. I'm Yuuta Asamura."

I matched her formal greeting, straightening my back without realizing it.

…She was in no way what I'd expected.

She clearly looked like the girl in the photo. If someone told me they were the same person, I'd be convinced immediately.

That is, if they said the photo was taken a decade ago.

Somewhat overwhelmed, I looked her over. This was no elementary schooler. This was a woman, through and through.

She had her long hair set neatly and not in some bizarre style, but the color was flashy, and she wore jewelry on her wrists and had pierced ears. Her top covered only one shoulder, though it wasn't vulgar or indecent. The restaurant lighting made it hard to tell, but she was probably wearing full makeup.

She was trendy and modern, fully armed with the latest fashion. An outgoing high school girl of the kind I hadn't ever expected to be involved with.

And yet she also seemed mature and sensible—perfectly comfortable meeting me for the first time. I felt uneasy, as if she had done up her buttons a little wrong.

I wasn't sure what to say as I sat down in the booth.

"Hey, this isn't what you told me," I whispered to my dad.

"I was surprised when I met her today, too. She was in elementary school in that photo."

"Seriously. She's gotta be my age."

"She is. She's turning sixteen this year. She's a second-year high school student."

"Sounds like she's not my *younger* sister at all."

"Your birthday is a week earlier than hers."

"Only one week."

Just a week. No matter what my dad said, we were the same age. The image of a worry-free life with an easygoing kid sister shattered to pieces in my mind.

"Sorry for the confusion," said Akiko. "Once she grew up, Saki stopped letting me take photos of her, and that old picture was the only one I could show you."

With a hand at her cheek, Akiko glanced at her daughter as if she didn't know what to do with her. She seemed to have guessed what Dad and I were whispering about.

I wasn't fond of getting my photo taken, either, so I could understand. The thing that baffled me was why Akiko had shown Dad a picture of her daughter as a little girl when she first told him about her. It was like she had no common sense.

"I'm not photogenic. I always look like I'm angry," said Ayase.

"Oh, um, okay."

Saki—no, I didn't want to get too familiar—Ayase smiled like she was embarrassed.

She had a pretty face by conventional beauty standards. I could understand why a guy like me, who wasn't particularly good-looking, wouldn't want his picture taken, but it didn't make much sense for her. I decided to keep that thought to myself, though. I wasn't going to push my preconceptions about what pretty girls did or didn't like on her.

Ayase pressed a hand to her chest.

"This is such a relief."

"What do you mean?" I asked.

"We're going to be living together, so I wasn't sure what I'd do if you turned out to be scary."

"Oh, I don't know. The scariest people look nice on the outside."

"Taichi was just telling us about you. He said you work part-time practically every day, and you're saving up for college. You sound like a pretty serious person."

"Actually, just ten minutes ago, my senior coworker got mad at me for being irresponsible."

"Your dad said you get good grades at school, too."

"A lot of criminals are smart."

"Ah-ha-ha."

Ayase daintily put a hand to her mouth and giggled.

Dad and Akiko, watching us nervously, smiled in relief.

My first meeting with my stepsister went relatively smoothly.

It was pretty different from what I'd rehearsed in my mind beforehand, but I thought I did a good job adapting. By the looks of things, I thought we could manage a nice, neutral relationship.

That first gathering of the Asamuras and the Ayases continued amicably, and we decided to call it a night a little after ten, since we all had to start early the next day.

Dad and Akiko said they would use the restroom and pay the check, so Ayase and I went outside to wait for them.

The Dogenzaka area of Shibuya was lively even late at night. After taking in the scenery—loud, drunk men, women in gaudy clothes, and workers calling customers into their shops—I glanced at my stepsister beside me.

She was clad in an eye-catching outfit, no different from those passing by. Exactly the kind of girl I thought I'd never be involved with.

But our conversation inside the restaurant had given me a sense of her deep intellect.

You couldn't judge a book by its cover. Appearance had nothing to do with a person's personality or manners, though it'd be kind of nice if it was that simple.

Still, I sensed something more behind her friendly attitude, an uneasiness that I found hard to describe.

And it wasn't long before I found out what it was.

"Hey, Asamura," she said. "I want to talk before our parents come out."

"Is there something you can't tell them?"

"Yeah. To be specific, it's something I can only tell you."

"I won your trust with just that brief conversation? Wow, I must be amazing."

"I can tell from the way you talk and joke around and your expression that you're pretty chill. That's why I think you'll totally understand what I'm about to say."

"Oh…"

That made sense. Basically, she was like me. That would explain the uneasiness I'd been feeling.

And that's when she said it. Looking back, her words must have set the tone for our relationship as siblings.

"I won't expect anything from you, and I don't want you to expect anything from me."

"You understand exactly what I mean by that, right?" she asked.

I saw my face steadily reflected in her eyes as she waited for my response.

Of course, my answer was clear.

Her words might have sounded like a cold "stay away from me" to some people, but to me, it was the most honest proposal I could imagine.

"I'm relieved to hear you say that," I replied. "I can finally relax."

"Yeah. Me too."

"We'll stick to that rule, then, Ayase."

"Thanks, Asamura."

And that's how I, Yuuta Asamura, and my stepsister, Saki Ayase, began our relationship as stepsiblings.

# ● JUNE 7 (SUNDAY)

"'Welcome to our home!' …That's not quite right… 'We'll be living under the same roof now, huh?!' …No, that sounds a little creepy. Hmm."

Eyeing the piles of boxes on the floor and the brand-new furniture that had arrived the day before, I stared into the mirror and practiced my lines like some kind of one-man show.

It was five in the evening.

I was sitting in one of the rooms in our third-floor apartment, located in Japan's most upscale neighborhood (okay, that might be a bit of an exaggeration).

Our place had three bedrooms, a living area, dining room, and kitchen. It had felt too big for just my dad and me, but starting today, it would be a little cramped. How would I greet the new members of our family, arriving any moment? That was what I'd been contemplating for the last five minutes.

Things had already started off on the wrong foot.

It made sense that Dad would prepare the room he and Akiko would use.

But to have me, a teenage guy, help set up a room for a girl I'd just met the day before? Even if she was going to be my little sister, wasn't that kind of insensitive?

"Oh, crap," said my dad. "Where did that thing go?"

"What's the matter?"

Dad was walking back and forth in the hallway, mumbling and looking troubled.

"Oh, there you are. Do you know where the Febreze is?"

"I think it's in the living room. I left it there after using it on the drapes yesterday."

"Oh, the living room! Thanks!"

Dad slapped his slippers noisily against the floor and hurried to the living room.

"What's with the last-minute rush?"

"I left the bedroom for last, but once I started, I got worried about the smell... I'd be devastated if Akiko thought I stank..."

"Are you that sensitive?"

"It's a critical issue at my age! You're still young, but give it twenty years, and you'll be just like me."

"I feel like you're cursing me."

I watched Dad run into his and Akiko's future bedroom, clutching a bottle of Febreze, and sighed.

*If you're that worried*, I thought, *then clean every day; don't wait until the last minute.* But I supposed that was a bit much to ask of a busy office worker.

"My room's okay...right?"

I was starting to get a little worried.

I'd promised Ayase that we wouldn't expect anything from each other, but I wasn't so short on common sense that I'd ask her to come into a room that smelled like a male high schooler on her first day in the house. But on the other hand, I'd cleaned it, washed the sheets, and sprayed everything with Febreze, so unless my nose was broken, it should be okay.

I was sitting there, happy with the results of the past few days, when the doorbell rang.

...They were finally here.

"Yuuta! Will you get that?"

"Coming!"

I half ran to the door in place of my dad. It seemed he didn't know when to give up and was still holding the Febreze, spraying away.

"Hello ther— Huh?"

I had intended to be friendly and cheerful.

But the perfect smile on my face froze the moment I opened the door.

Akiko stood there, holding several department-store shopping bags in both hands.

The bags were so stuffed, things were spilling out of them, including a huge leg of prosciutto. Everything seemed to have a big, exaggerated presence.

"Uh, Akiko. What is all that…?"

"I bought these to thank you for taking us in!"

"So much? You didn't have to."

"Don't worry. It's not what you think," said an exasperated voice from behind Akiko.

It was Saki—no, Ayase. She was also holding paper bags in both hands, and she sounded exhausted.

"Mom has a hard time saying no, so she bought everything the sales clerk recommended."

"Oh, I see…," I replied.

"Hey," Akiko cut in. "You're making me sound like a useless adult."

"You are, though," Ayase shot back.

"What?! That's not true, is it, Yuuta?!"

Now I was being dragged into it.

Personally, as I stared at the leg of prosciutto, I thought Akiko sounded like a pushover. But all that vanished from my mind when she looked at me with a childish pout.

That didn't mean I was ready to lie and say she didn't have a problem, though. Ayase's eyes were silently telling me, "Don't pamper her." I felt like middle management, stuck between mother and daughter with no good options.

"Come on in," I said. "I'll take your bags."

I figured ignoring them was the best option. A wise person once said the ability to ignore is indispensable for achieving happiness.

Akiko handed me the paper bags and smiled sweetly, unbothered by my change of topic.

"Thank you. It's nice to have a man around."

"Ah-ha-ha."

I flashed her a neutral smile, turned on my heel, and offered them both newly bought slippers as I invited them inside.

Akiko cooed in joy as soon as she stepped into the living room.

"Mmm, it smells fresh and citrusy."

"Wow, you keep the place pretty clean," said Ayase.

She also appeared impressed and exhaled. The air was fresh, and the wooden floor had been polished to a shine.

"We did a rush cleaning job," I began. "It isn't usually—"

"It's just like Taichi said," Akiko interrupted. "You two do like to keep things clean."

"—They say you need a healthy environment to nurture a healthy mind," I finished, swallowing my denial and quickly agreeing instead.

That was close. Dad had been telling Akiko good things about us to impress her. Of course, it would serve him right if she found out the truth and her impression of him went down the drain, but I felt bad getting in his way when he was finally recovering from his old wounds and trying to be happy. For now, I decided to go along with it.

Meanwhile, Ayase was staring at me like she thought something was up.

"Do you always keep the place this clean?" she asked.

"Oh yeah, of course. It's our family motto to exterminate everything without leaving a speck of dust."

"That sounds kind of scary."

I was telling the truth. My grandmother out in the country was always saying those words came from one of our ancestors—some lord from the Warring States period. I recalled smiling as I listened to her and thinking that it was almost certainly a lie.

"But wow, Taichi truly is amazing," Akiko said, smiling. "I know he pays a lot of attention to his appearance, but even his home is wonderful."

"His appearance...?" I asked. "You're talking about my dad, right?"

"Of course! The first time he came to our bar, he seemed down-to-earth, probably because he was there with his boss. After that, he always wore lovely cologne and a nice tie from a high-end brand like an elite businessman."

"Oh, I see."

Come to think of it, there was a period when Dad started spending a lot on clothes and cologne. At the time, I'd told myself it was just the price of participating in adult society. I'd never imagined he was trying to woo a woman.

"H-hey, Akiko. Saki!"

Just then, Dad came out of his bedroom. The spray bottle of air freshener in his hand had just revealed his middle-school-level ploy to impress. I froze.

"D-Dad…"

*Put that away already*, I thought. *I'm doing my best to go along with your plan. Don't show off the evidence.*

Since I couldn't tell him out loud, I tried to communicate through eye contact. But my efforts were in vain, and he flashed a smile I was sure he must have practiced a hundred times in front of his mirror.

"Welcome to our home! W-we'll be living under the same roof now, and w-we're going to h-have a w-wonderful life together!"

A home run. He'd said it all—a veritable exhibition of cringe.

His wording was creepy, he stuttered, he tried too hard to sound enthusiastic, and the practiced look on his face was almost painful to see.

"Thank you for the big welcome!" Akiko exclaimed. "Here, this is from me!"

"A whole leg of prosciutto? Mmm. We'll have a real party tonight!"

They were an easy-to-please couple if that was all it took to get their spirits up.

Akiko hadn't noticed the Febreze, and Dad was fine with all the bags she had brought. They were both a little odd, but maybe that made them a good match.

"Hey, Asamura?" Ayase said.

"Hmm?"

"Will you show me to my room? I'd like to see it."

"Oh, um, yeah… Okay."

Leaving the adults and their weird, cheery atmosphere behind, Ayase and I put the department-store shopping bags in the living area and headed to her room.

"This is it," I said.

"Wow…"

"We set up the bed and curtains, but we didn't know what color sheets you liked, so you can change them if you want. I thought a desk by the window would be typical, but tell me if you want it moved someplace else."

"Thanks. You really went to the trouble to set everything up for me… I'm impressed."

She slipped past me and walked into the middle of the room. Though her tone was flat, her eyes were busy taking in her surroundings like a curious cat.

A girl my age was standing right in front of me. She was a rare beauty, with her brightly dyed hair and fashionable appearance. I wasn't sure if it was her shampoo, pheromones, or some special power at work that a virgin like me couldn't understand, but a sweet scent like roasted honey permeated the air.

She turned around, that scent lingering in her wake.

"It's so spacious," she said.

"Is it? I think it's pretty standard."

"Our last place was a shabby studio apartment. I didn't even have my own room."

"Oh, so you and Akiko had to spread out futons every night…or something?"

No wonder all the furniture looked new.

"Not exactly. I had the place to myself at night. I went to school during the day, and my mom worked at night, so our routines were completely reversed."

"It must have been pretty carefree living like that, though. Now you're going to have to deal with two extra guys in the house. I apologize for the inconvenience."

"...That's okay, but...can I ask you something?"

"Of course. What is it?"

"The way you talk."

"Huh?"

"Why do you sound so formal? Not that I want you to change your beliefs or principles or anything."

Did she think I was in some weird cult? I guess I did unquestioningly accept the idea that you should be polite to people you were meeting for the first time or those of higher rank, which might be some kind of Japanese religious thing I wasn't aware of. But that aside...

"I'm actually not sure...," I said.

"We're the same age. You can be casual with me. You don't have to go out of your way to be polite."

"That's all the more reason to be formal."

"Huh? Isn't it weird to talk to your friends and classmates like they're above you?"

"That kind of attitude is for outgoing, successful people."

In my sixteen years, I'd barely ever talked to girls, particularly eye-catching ones like Ayase. It might sound easy to her, but it wasn't so simple for me to act casual and friendly.

"You think so?" she asked. "Well, I won't complain, but you don't have to try to please me if that's what this is."

"No, it's not about that... Oh."

A thought occurred to me midsentence.

I recalled the day we first met when we were leaving the restaurant. Ayase had suggested we not expect anything from each other.

*No expectations.* I repeated these words in my mind as I posed a question to her.

"To make things clear, I want to ask you directly: Would you prefer if I wasn't...formal with you?"

"Yeah, it would be easier if we could be casual. I mean, I'm not someone you have to respect."

"Okay. Got it."

I shrugged, dropping my formal tone.

Ayase's eyes widened in surprise.

"That was quick."

"I gotta admit, it isn't easy to talk to you like we're old friends, but it's the least I can do, since you're being so straightforward. As long as you're up front with me, everything will be easier."

"Aha. I thought so."

She smiled. It felt like my first peek at a softer side to her beneath the flat, cold-as-concrete impression she usually gave off.

"It's nice that we can hash things out like this," she said.

"Hashing things out, huh? That's a good way to put it."

She was right. That's exactly what this exchange was.

Ayase had thrown me the ball first by suggesting that I didn't have to be formal while leaving room for me to decline in case I had some special religious belief. Then I tossed the ball back into her court by checking what she preferred, and we settled on neutral ground based on her positive reply.

You might have thought that sounded like a perfectly simple and normal conversation. But it was actually my first time going over something so smoothly.

In most cases, humans seek understanding and empathy from others:

"You should understand how I feel even if I don't explain myself!" "Why can't you see that what you're saying irritates me?!"

...As if a person could look inside someone else's brain. Humans always expect so much from each other.

It's easier to lay out all the cards at the start:

"If you say x, y, or z, I'll get angry." "This thing is really important to me." "I see. In that case, let's do things this way."

Exchange information about yourselves, not because you're hoping for mutual understanding, but to give each other an idea of how best to get along.

"Things would be easy if the whole of humanity could just be chill, like you and me," Ayase said.

"Well, yeah, but that's not how it works."

I didn't understand her sensitivity to formal language. But as long as I knew it was something she didn't like, I could avoid pointlessly stressing her out.

All it took was a practical, mechanical approach.

If everyone went over their emotions with honesty and figured out their differences, they could all be happy. But for some reason, that wasn't how the world worked.

"My friends at school don't take me seriously when I talk like this," she said. "Instead, they laugh and ask me if I'm trying to get them to sign some kind of agreement."

"That sounds tough."

"Yeah. So I cut ties with all but one person."

"Wow, that's... Geez."

That sounded like quite a bold, daring move. But the way she laughed cheerfully as she told me about it was strangely refreshing.

"They were all people I didn't mind losing," she continued. "Trying to get on their good side seemed like a waste of time when I had no idea what they were thinking or when they might explode."

"Point taken... Oh, speaking of time, standing here's kind of a waste. Want me to help you sort out your stuff?"

"That's nice of you."

"You might repay me one day, so it's a win-win."

"I see you've thought this through."

"I wish you'd stop teasing me..."

"I meant that as a compliment. Okay, where should we start?"

She looked around the room, thinking it over, then started mumbling to herself.

"I guess I gotta start with *that*. Otherwise, we won't get anywhere," she said, pointing to a cardboard box. "I'd like to put that one away first. Do you have a box cutter?"

"Yeah, sure."

I went to my room, got a box cutter from my desk drawer, and approached the cardboard box she'd pointed to.

"Oh, just hand it to me. I'll do it," she said.

"Don't worry, it's no trouble opening a box."

"That isn't what I meant. It's just that…"

Ayase seemed to want to say something, but I had my back to her and was already slicing through the masking tape. There was a loud ripping sound, and I saw white material in the box. I understood her reaction then and regretted what I had done.

"That box contains…clothes," she said.

"I wish you would have told me that sooner!"

I averted my eyes from what I had just seen and backed away, panicking. Ayase chuckled at my reaction. It must've been obvious I was a virgin.

"Ah-ha-ha. You don't have to treat it like it's contaminated," she said. "That's a little insulting."

"Don't you know how tempting stuff like that is for a teenage guy?"

"It might be if I was wearing it, but once it's washed, it's not that different from a handkerchief."

"Oh no, don't hold it up like that. *Please.*"

She pulled out the white cloth and playfully fluttered it in the air. I knew it was only a piece of fabric, but it made me oddly anxious.

We were on the same page regarding interpersonal relationships, but it appeared we had some major differences.

"I'll handle my underwear," she said. "Would you mind hanging up my school uniform?"

"Uniforms are pretty provocative, too," I shot back.

"Settle down. If you get excited by everything, you won't be able to help. Come on, don't think. Just work."

"R-right. Don't think. Okay."

I repeated the words and picked up her uniform, which consisted of a shirt, skirt, and cardigan. I couldn't help noticing how soft everything felt.

"Huh?"

My hands stopped moving. The tie, probably designated by the school, was a distinctive light green—the color of young leaves. As soon as it entered my field of vision, I was overwhelmed by a powerful sense of déjà vu.

"Hey...Ayase. Is this from Suisei by any chance?"

"Yeah. Are you surprised that a flashy girl like me goes to a prep school like Suisei?"

"That's not why I'm surprised... I go there, too."

Suisei Metropolitan High School was a school in Tokyo's Shibuya district for elite students. It took pride in its alumni's high rate of enrollment in top colleges. The curriculum was strict, but students were allowed to take part-time jobs if they kept up their grades, and that flexibility was what had appealed to me when I'd chosen a school.

Talk about a strange twist of fate. My dad remarried, and I wound up with a stepsister who was not only my age but also went to my school. At least she wasn't in my class. That would have been *truly* awkward.

I looked at Ayase to gauge her reaction and saw her narrowing her eyes beneath her feathery bangs. She appeared to be thinking.

"So you go to Suisei, too...," she said. "I see..."

"...I'm sorry. Dad should have checked beforehand."

"There's nothing for you to be sorry about. Mom didn't check, either."

"But it'll be awkward. I'll just pretend I don't know you when we're at school."

"Huh? No, that's okay. Though, maybe you'll be more comfortable that way."

"What do you mean by—?"

I swallowed the rest of my sentence when my phone suddenly started vibrating. I pulled it out and checked the screen, which said simply, **Work**.

"Go ahead and take the call. I'm not interested in tying you down, and it doesn't bug me if you talk on the phone in front of me."

"We really do think alike," I said, meaning it from the bottom of my heart.

I tapped the TALK button as I left Ayase's room. A call at this hour probably meant they wanted me to fill in for someone who couldn't work their shift. It turned out exactly as I'd thought, and though I was annoyed, I agreed to help out. I was a real yes-man.

I finished my call and went back to Ayase's room, where she was still unpacking. I saw her turn to me, looking bored.

"What did they want?" she asked.

"They want me to fill in for someone at work. Sorry, I won't be able to help you anymore."

"That's okay. It's my job anyway."

Ayase wasn't the least bit bothered by the sudden change in plans. She took it in stride, like this was all business as usual.

A beautiful girl my age, with a flashy, rebellious appearance. From my point of view, she had all the elements of a ticking time bomb—exactly what I didn't want. But because of her mature attitude, I was able to talk with her with minimal anxiety.

"Okay, then," I said. "I'm off."

"See you."

Her tone was matter-of-fact, and she went right back to work. She was nothing like what you might expect from a *younger sister*. But she was the most comforting type of person I could have asked for as a new member of my family, and I left the room relieved.

I was at a large bookstore near Shibuya Station.

It was located just past Shibuya Crossing outside the Hachiko exit, which was always full of tourists and YouTubers shooting videos with tripods and selfie sticks.

Looking up at the large display screen blasting commercials about smartphone games at maximum volume, I parked my bicycle and walked into the eight-floor building where I worked.

My part-time job was here at this bookstore.

I'd always been a bookworm and devoured everything from children's books to foreign literature, even mysteries and fantasies, until they lost all their flavor. I don't read; I devour. That's the best way to put it. And the bookstore where I work, filled with the fresh paper smell of newly printed books, was pure heaven.

Books are great. They allow us a peek into all sorts of other people's lives. Normally, the only life that I, Yuuta Asamura, could experience would be the boring, average day-to-day of a regular guy. But when I read, I could share in the lives of countless other people.

I'm not just talking about fiction. Autobiographies are the same way, and so are books about business. Through books, you can download all sorts of people into your mind.

Books about tunnel vision, for instance. Or careless negligence. Or the type of narcissism that makes you want to cover your face in discomfort.

Maybe it's because I've read so many books that I've become able to think metacognitively and look at myself from an objective point of view so I don't end up embarrassing myself with issues like that.

An adult male brain weighs about fourteen hundred grams.

When I think about that, I feel scared to live my life based only on the "common sense" of such a tiny, closed space and the decisions it makes.

*If I didn't read*, I wondered, *would I have ended up like the people in those books?*

It was now eight PM.

I'd come to help around six, and two hours had passed. I'd been dealing with customers and working the cash register during the busiest time for the weekend.

The number of people in the store was finally dwindling, and I was folding book covers at the register hoping for a little breather, when a particular scene caught my attention.

"Damn, lady, you are seriously my type. This has to be love at first sight."

"Are you looking for a particular book?"

"Huh? Man, you're *too* cute. How about dinner after you finish work? What time do you get off?"

"As they say, *take a hike.*"

"God, I have no idea what you're saying, but you're so funny!"

The guy bothering the female clerk was one of those noisy partygoer types. She was snubbing him, but he wasn't getting it. You often came across interactions like this in Shibuya, though it was rare to witness so persistent a pickup attempt aimed at a bookstore employee right in her place of work.

The victim was the picture of a delicate Japanese beauty with impressive long black hair. She was a neat, lovely girl who was clearly into literature—the total opposite of a flirt. She was like a flower, spreading a gentle aroma into the air around her.

Despite the rude, flippant behavior of the guy trying to hit on her, she maintained a graceful, businesslike smile, though her eyes were cold.   .

*I don't want any trouble, but...*

I picked up a random binder and a list and proceeded to the source of the commotion.

"Uh, Yomiuri," I said, addressing the woman. "There's something I want to ask you."

"Oh, okay!" she replied "What do you need?"

"Our new shipment list doesn't look right, but I don't know how to compare it to the information on the computer."

"...! Okay, I'll take a look right away."

"Wha—? Hey, wait a sec!" the guy called out.

Aware of what I was doing, the female clerk tried to escape, but the man panicked and reached out to grab her. His rough hands moved for her delicate wrists, but I casually blocked his fingertips with the binder.

"Do you need something else from my girlfriend?" I asked.

"Huh?" the man said, confused.

Of course, she and I weren't in a relationship or anything. This was just a lie to get through the situation.

The man's mouth hung open, and he froze for a moment; then he clapped his hands and bowed low.

"Oh, geez, sorry, I didn't realize...! Right, of course! A pretty girl like her couldn't possibly be single."

"What? Oh, um, right."

He'd taken me by surprise.

In the world of fiction, guys like him usually got furious and threw a punch at you, but I guess things were different in real life.

Or maybe it was just him.

"Hey, take good care of her, mister. Best wishes!"

He even went so far as to give us his blessings, struck a cliché pose typical of guys like him, and left the store.

With the noisy customer gone, it was quiet once again. I suddenly became aware of the other customers eyeing me and quickly returned to the register, head low as I tried to hide the blush that had spread to my ears.

"Thanks, Yuuta," said Yomiuri. "You saved the day. But that flirt... If he was going to give up that easily, he should have backed off when I snubbed him... Don't you agree, *boyfriend*?"

"Stop that."

"We were an item for only one minute—not even a one-night stand! Boo-hoo."

Yomiuri's business smile disappeared when she returned to the register. She stuck out her tongue and chuckled devilishly. Then she pulled her name tag out from a pocket and attached it to the right side of her uniform.

"Aren't we supposed to keep our name tags on during our shift...?"

"We have to be flexible."

Yomiuri touched her delicate index finger to her lips, indicating that I should keep this our secret.

"Rules exist so an organization can function smoothly," she said. "But it'll be even worse if a guy like that finds out my name and keeps coming back like a pain in the ass."

"That's true."

Yomiuri must have been super smart. Instead of following the rules to the letter, she understood their purpose and acted accordingly. To me, this intelligence was her most appealing trait, but a lot of other guys didn't seem to agree.

"This is the third time this month," I said.

"Today's the seventh, which makes it once every other day."

She put on a show of sinking weakly to the floor behind the cash register where the customers wouldn't see her.

Someone else might think she was humblebragging by complaining about how often customers tried to put the moves on her, but my policy was to remain neutral, so I was able to listen to her honest worries without any strange biases.

"I wish they'd at least move it somewhere else," I said. "Since you tease me every time I cover for you... Though, I guess I've gotten used to it by now."

"I appreciate it. You're a really dependable guy, Yuuta."

"...Oh, sorry. I wasn't fishing for compliments."

"That's okay. I'm causing you trouble, so fish away."

She laughed and patted me on the shoulder.

Yomiuri looked like a delicate Japanese beauty, but she let her guard down when we had shifts alone together. She'd even start cracking jokes with me.

At first, I was shocked by her lack of restraint and how she'd casually touch me, but it was easy to get used to once I realized that was just how she was and she was only being friendly.

"But you sure are popular with the guys," I remarked. "I guess it's because you're beautiful."

"Oh, Yuuta...don't be so quick to compliment me, or you'll wind up like that customer someday."

"Please don't scare me."

"But I don't think those guys come after me because they think I'm beautiful. They probably just figure I'd be an easy lay."

"An easy...lay...?"

The straightforward way she said it, with no forewarning, made me choke.

Yomiuri was beautiful, but she was also graceful and reserved.

Those features made her an outcast in Shibuya, and maybe they gave some guys the wrong impression...

I knew well that the idea of a pure, naive, inexperienced young lady who was therefore easy to have your way with was only a sad male fantasy. The real deal tended to be pretty harsh and even sadistic. For example:

"By the way, I've been smelling girl on you all day," Yomiuri said. "What's the deal? Are you seeing someone?"

"Don't be silly… Um, do I really smell like girl?"

"Oh yeah. It's pungent. I wonder how much intense flirting it would take to make you smell like that."

"I'm leaving early. I'll go home and take a shower."

"Hey, I was only kidding. Don't leave me here by myself!" Yomiuri cried, clinging to me as I sniffed the sleeve of my uniform and pretended to make my way out the door.

Yomiuri and I were the only ones there. Peak hours had passed, but managing the rest of the shift alone would have been tough. Of course, I was only joking and wasn't seriously considering going home.

"You told me something before about a stepsister moving in with you," she said.

"Oh yeah."

That's right, I had discussed the matter with her previously.

When I learned that Ayase and I were the same age, I wasn't sure what kind of distance was appropriate, and I'd asked Yomiuri for advice as my only real female acquaintance who I felt comfortable talking to.

She'd found the whole thing amusing. All she did was tease me; she didn't offer any useful advice.

"*I can't say anything, since all you've told me is that she's a girl. Different people have different personalities, interests, and values,*" she'd said. Her argument sounded convincing, and I wasn't about to complain.

"How is she? Is she cute?" Yomiuri asked.

"I don't think it's right to look at her that way."

"I know you aren't the type of lech who'd be over the moon to have a girl move in with him. I'm just asking you for an objective observation."

"…Beautiful… I think she's beautiful," I answered honestly.

My words were muddled because I felt uneasy and a little guilty talking that way about someone of the opposite sex who would be living with me as part of my family.

We might take similar positions on interpersonal relationships, but I wasn't so brazen as to start telling people that Ayase and I were close. We were hardly living on the same planet.

Ayase had a nice figure and a great face, dyed her hair a pretty gold color, and was fashionable, wearing clothes and jewelry that suited her perfectly. She was positive and outgoing, too. Obviously not an introvert like I was.

I wouldn't be surprised if she thought compliments from a shy weirdo like me were not only unpleasant but downright gross.

"Good job, tiger!" Yomiuri said. "So you'll be living with a hottie. Spring has come."

"Nothing is going to happen."

"*Something* could happen."

"Stop it. You sound like a dirty old man."

"I can't help it. I went to all-girls schools from junior high straight through college."

"Are you trying to ruin their reputation…?"

"But that's really how they are."

"…Seriously?"

"It's up to you whether to believe it or not… Ha-ha."

Yomiuri winked playfully like she was reciting the opening line from some TV show about urban legends. I mentally chose not to believe her. I wanted to preserve the sacred image in my heart of all-girls schools being lily-filled gardens of learning.

"I'm a healthy young guy, so sure, there are moments when I start imagining things. But I honestly don't think it's the time to have evil thoughts."

"Hmm?"

"Think about it. I'm living under the same roof as a girl my age. That's a huge challenge for a guy like me who has zero experience with the opposite sex."

"What do you think I am, exactly?"

"You're more like a guy."

"Ah-ha-ha! Hey, that's going too far! That said, you're probably right."

"You're like a male friend to me—an older guy I can depend on."

I mean, she even told dirty jokes... Though, it was possible women were even nastier than men when it came to stuff like that.

"Ah-ha-ha-ha. Wow... *Pfft*. Ha-ha-ha... Okay, I got it. I can tell by what you just said that your skills with girls are disastrous."

"...I won't deny it or make excuses."

I couldn't even if I wanted to.

"I'm seriously unsure what attitude I should take as her stepsibling," I continued. "How should I treat her? I'm up to my neck with things to worry about, so I don't have the time to be happy about living with a beautiful girl."

"I think you'll be okay if you just act natural."

"But won't she dislike me?"

"Do you dislike me when I act natural?"

"...Not at all."

"See?"

"But you're beautiful... Someone beautiful acting natural and an introvert like me acting natural are two totally different things."

"Your self-esteem is way too low. I like you just fine, Yuuta."

"But you're weird..."

"Oh-ho! Way to one-eighty. That's good. Artistic."

"See, that's exactly what I mean."

Yomiuri instantly takes on the persona of a professional critic when she likes something I say. According to her, it's a special move just for book-loving girls. Apparently, she's always looking for beautiful rhetoric hidden in our daily lives.

In effect, this was no different from middle-aged men thinking up corny jokes every second of the day, but I decided to keep that cruel truth locked away in my heart.

As I stood there, sadly contemplating the similarities between a beautiful literature afficionado and a perverted old man, Yomiuri remembered something and ran to the sales floor.

She returned a short while later, holding a book in her hands.

"Found it. Here, I suggest you read this," she said.

"*The Chemistry of Men and Women*?"

"It talks about ways to befriend others—particularly those of the opposite sex—based on psychological studies. I use it as a reference, too."

"It looks interesting."

That was my honest reaction as I flipped through the pages. I glanced at the table of contents and instantly felt I needed to read this book.

First, it said, you should get to know the other person.

Then you should get to know yourself.

And in order to do that, you should learn to see yourself objectively.

Other books I'd read said similar things. That's why I'd always striven to live my life while seeing myself objectively. This was nothing particularly new.

But one line in the table of contents drew my attention:

"Keep a diary if you want to improve your ability to see objectively!"

This advice was specific and immediately achievable. That alone made me interested in checking out the book.

Since reading was my hobby, I often came across works similar to others I'd read in the past, and because they discussed the same topics, I was able to enjoy the characteristics of each author and the different ways they addressed things.

Perhaps Yomiuri could tell that the table of contents interested me. She flashed me an evil grin like a succubus.

"I might already have proven how effective this book is on you," she said.

"You've been using it on me?"

"Are you convinced yet? You and I get along just fine."

"There's nothing more credible than that."

A simple action is better than a hundred hypotheses.

An overweight person who quietly continues to put effort into losing excess fat is far smarter than one who simply uses a bunch of fancy words to talk about the joys of dieting.

So in the end, I decided to buy the book.

After finishing my shift and shedding my uniform in the changing room, I purchased *The Chemistry of Men and Women* from Yomiuri, who would be on the late shift until midnight. She was lamenting that, unlike me, a kid who could work until only ten, she had a long night ahead of her.

I accepted the book, which was wrapped in a freshly folded cover, then slipped it into my bag. I was about to leave when I turned around one last time.

"Call me whenever another guy gives you trouble," I said. "I'll come charging here on my bicycle."

Yomiuri looked stunned for a minute; then her face melted into a smile.

"A guy I can count on. ♪ Okay, I'll call you and then the police if that happens."

"I'd rather you called the police first."

If she called the cops, then she'd have no need for me.

It was past ten PM when I reached the bicycle parking lot at our apartment.

It had taken me longer than usual to get home because I'd been searching for a diary app Yomiuri had recommended. I'd downloaded it while pushing my bicycle up the road.

I parked my beloved bike in an empty space and suddenly felt guilty as I took the elevator up to the third floor.

I had come home at my own pace as usual, but I'd suddenly realized that I hadn't told Akiko or Ayase when I would finish my shift.

If I was lucky, Dad would have filled them in, but it wasn't in his nature to notice subtle things like that.

Figuring it was possible everyone was already asleep, I opened the door quietly and tiptoed into the living room. Then I saw that the lights were on beyond the frosted glass door. Someone was still awake.

I straightened my back a bit and stepped into the living room.

There she was: Ayase, seated alone on the sofa.

She was sipping from a cup of— Was it hot chocolate? A sweet scent wafted over to me as she raised it to her mouth, smartphone in one hand, her face devoid of expression. Was she texting a friend? A boyfriend? Either seemed possible for a pretty, fashionable, outgoing girl like her.

"I'm home," I said.

"Huh? Oh, hi."

She raised her head and offered a half-hearted response.

She seemed more confused than like she was trying to brush me off, and she glanced blankly in my direction as if some foreigner had asked her directions in a language she didn't understand.

"...Ayase?"

"Sorry. It's rare for someone to greet me when they get home, so I didn't know what to say."

"Oh...right, because you and your mom were on different schedules."

Come to think of it, I recalled Ayase saying she and her mom slept at different hours.

I didn't dwell too much on it at the time, figuring that was just normal for some families, but her confusion over a simple greeting like that tugged at my heart.

"Ha-ha. You look so serious," Ayase said, smiling wryly.

Apparently, she saw right through me.

"It's okay," she continued. "It's not like I was being mistreated or anything. Mom slept and did things around the house while I went to school, and she was at work by the time I came home... That was our routine."

"The two of you look so close."

"We're mother and daughter. We went shopping together today for the first time in a while, and it was pretty fun."

She said all this without emotion, and her face remained expressionless.

Listening to her talk about her family, I was starting to understand why she looked so calm and mature. She probably showed no hint of loneliness because she was simply used to being alone.

She'd been raised in a single-parent family, but she was already in high school. I was the same way. We were well past the age where we might make a big deal about missing our parents.

But all that aside, though I still didn't know if she was texting a friend or a boyfriend, I'd interrupted her while she was doing something on her phone. I started feeling guilty and decided to hurry to my room.

"I'm going to take a bath and go to bed."

"Go ahead. I'll take a bath after you're finished. I like being the last to bathe and go to bed."

"Oh, okay."

I obediently did as I was told and got ready for a soak in the tub, all the while thinking over what she'd just said.

She liked being the last to bathe and the last to go to bed.

It was our first day living together, and I couldn't blame her. I was a guy her age, and she'd only just met me. She probably didn't want me to soak in a tub after she'd used it or take a chance of having me see her asleep and unguarded.

I might have been keeping her up.

In that case...I'd try to finish up as quickly as I could.

With that decided, I finished bathing in ten minutes—much quicker than the half hour I usually spent in the bathroom. The next twenty minutes went to draining and washing the tub, after which I refilled it for her.

I wasn't sure yet how best to handle Ayase, but I wanted to use my head and be as considerate as possible.

And just for your information...

Though I was spending the night under the same roof with a girl my age for the first time, I didn't experience any exciting, suggestive scenes like you often saw in romantic comedies aimed at boys. Living with a step-sister in real life isn't like what you read in those two-dimensional comic books, just like I said at the beginning.

However, the real reason I was able to sleep without thinking at all about Ayase must have been because she never once let down her guard like you might expect someone to do at home. At least not until after I was unconscious.

The next morning, she was sitting in the living room by the time I got up, perfectly poised, giving me no chances to get excited, but...

"Good morning," she said. "Did you sleep well?"

"Yep."

"I enjoyed my bath last night. I appreciate you going to the trouble."

...through our exchange, I caught a glimpse of her human warmth—not the usual Ayase, who was always as cool as a cucumber. Our relationship wasn't like those comic-book fantasies, but I thought it was still pretty nice.

# ● JUNE 8 (MONDAY)

No special event, such as accompanying Ayase to school like it was our new daily routine, occurred that morning.

After learning that she went to Suisei, I had wondered if we might, but guess what? She calmly suggested that we act like total strangers for the time being so that people wouldn't gossip about us. There was no denying that she was right.

Dad and Akiko appeared to have considered this and left us with different surnames so our situations would stay the same.

If Ayase's name had changed, the resulting paperwork and suspicion from other students would have been a hassle, so that was a big relief.

Anyway, we left home at different times and went to school separately, both headed to Suisei Metropolitan High School.

Society was fiercely competitive, and in order to survive in this world, we needed to achieve results, both academically and in sports. That was our school's doctrine.

Suisei emphasized results over effort. Turning that around, it meant you wouldn't get in trouble if you got a part-time job or missed classes as long as you got good grades. That freedom was what had appealed to me when I chose this school.

Though I was attending an elite prep school, there wasn't a particular college I wanted to get into or a big goal I was working toward. I did want to enroll at a good college, but that wasn't because I was conscientious or had a positive attitude. On the contrary, all I'd been doing my whole life was avoiding anything that seemed like a hassle.

Once, when I was in elementary school, I was told to go to a cram school.

This was before my dad's divorce. The woman who had been my mother was determined to make me someone better than my dad, with more influence in society, and tried send me to a famous cram school.

...I started having problems during my trial admission.

It was surprisingly agonizing to be around and study with unfamiliar kids from other schools, and I actually felt like throwing up. It was the first time in my life that I realized I was an introvert.

So what did I do, you ask? Well, I studied so hard that I thought I'd die, and my grades rapidly improved. Now that I was attending a prep school, my rank was around the middle of the top half of my grade, but back in junior high, my grades were first-rate.

I didn't do any of this out of ambition, however. My efforts stemmed from a simple desire to stay away from cram school. It was all just a reaction—I was fleeing from the pressure I was under to attend those extra study sessions.

The only reason I was doing part-time work while putting in the effort to maintain my grades was to show Dad how independent I was. It'd be annoying if he worried about my future, so once again, I was simply doing it to avoid hassle.

That was why I had the deepest respect for genuinely conscientious, positive people who worked hard to achieve their goals. My best friend, Tomokazu Maru, was just such a person.

"Heya, Asamura."

"Hey, Maru. Did you have morning practice today?"

I was sitting in my classroom, waiting for school to start, when Maru arrived ten minutes before homeroom and sat heavily in the seat in front of me.

He wore glasses that made him look smart, and he had short, unruly hair and a meaty middle. People would take one look at his build and call him fat, but that wasn't the case. I, too, was surprised when I heard it was mostly muscle covering his huge body. I later learned that sumo wrestlers' bodies were also mostly muscle. You really can't judge a person by their appearance.

"That's a silly question. I always have morning practice," Maru said with a sour look on his face.

He was on the baseball team—the catcher, as you might guess from his looks. He was enthusiastic about playing baseball but wasn't too happy about having to attend practice day in, day out.

"Our baseball team is practically a sweatshop," he continued. "They expect you to come in early and stay late. There's abuse of power and seniority, not to mention infighting and jealousy. Merit hardly counts for anything. Frankly, they should call it and hand me the win already."

"You're winning in this scenario?"

"You raise a good point. But unless you truly love the sport, you lose the moment you join the team. Once you're in, the feeling of total exhaustion can really grow on you...but I don't expect an outsider like you to understand."

"Ugh. I could never handle that."

Maru took off his glasses and pulled their case out of his bag. Inside was another pair, which he took out and put on.

He said one was for sports and the other for schoolwork, and he would switch depending on what he was doing, as if he were a character in an RPG. He broke his glasses once during practice and had been carrying around an extra pair ever since.

"Oh, by the way, how's your new life?" Maru asked out of the blue.

I had told my best friend that my dad was getting remarried and that my family would be growing.

To be honest, I had barely any friends at school. It came down to how much trouble I had with meeting new people. After all, I was so antisocial that cram school had been a nightmare.

But Tomokazu Maru and I had sat near each other since we first entered high school, and because we were both interested in manga and anime, we'd talked a lot. Before I knew it, we'd become friends. You may think

it's weird for a jock to be into nerdy stuff, but it happened the other way around. Maru started the sport after reading a popular baseball manga, making him an "active geek" rather than an "introverted athlete." He was the type of nerd who would start going to a gym or get hooked on camping after seeing an anime on the topic.

So of course, I'd told Maru about my situation.

"My new family is… Well, to sum it up, they're different from what I expected."

"So I hear you have a sister now, huh? You're a big brother, you lucky dog."

"Don't say it like you're cursing me. Well…I mean, she's technically my little sister, but…"

"What, can't get excited if you're not blood-related?"

"I can't look at my sister that way, whether she's blood-related or a step-sibling. Besides," I added, conjuring Ayase's face in my mind, "she's more of a woman than a little sister."

"That sounds pretty perverted, if you ask me."

"That's the only way to describe her. I honestly don't know how to interact with her."

"Hmm, I see. A woman, huh? Well, they say grade-schoolers mature early these days."

"Grade-schoolers? What are you talking about?"

"We're talking about your sister, right?"

Maru blinked like he wanted to ask me what *I* was saying.

But wasn't that my line?

…No, wait a minute. Dad had told me I would have a younger sister, and I'd taken it for granted that she would be much younger than me, maybe still in elementary school or junior high. That was why it'd seemed perfectly natural when he'd shown me a picture of her from when she was little.

It would be perfectly natural for Maru to think the same thing.

"Hold on a second. First of all, my sister is—"

I stopped midsentence.

As it happened, my sister wasn't in elementary school. She was a high school student in the same grade at the same school as us. I didn't know which class she was in, but she was pretty… If I told Maru that, I'd make him curious. He might even start getting suspicious.

Maru was my best friend; I could probably trust him. But I couldn't break the promise I'd made with Ayase. Trust was paramount, and I wasn't a guy who blabbed.

"What about your sister?" Maru asked.

"My sister… Oh, she wasn't what I expected. She's completely different from the type you see in anime and manga."

"Of course she is. Have you finally lost touch with reality?"

"Don't say 'finally.' It makes it sound like I've been on the precipice for a while now."

"It's true, though, isn't it?"

"Just because something's true doesn't mean you should say it."

"But that's how I roll."

I knew that.

Maru and I had been friends for more than a year, and I knew his commentary could be razor-sharp and ruthless.

"Anyway," I said, "for the record, I don't find her the least bit exciting. It's actually pretty nerve-racking trying to figure out how to interact with her and how much distance to put between us."

"I can imagine."

"By the way, changing the subject completely…do you happen to know a student named Saki Ayase?"

"Huh? I've heard of her, but where did that come from?"

Maru furrowed his thick brows. He had no idea this was simply a continuation of the previous topic.

Guys on sports teams had big networks. I wouldn't be surprised if a girl—particularly one as pretty as Ayase—had come up in conversation, though I'd never heard rumors myself, since I wasn't interested in such topics. Maru, on the other hand, had once complained to me that he was fed up with hearing stories about girls he wasn't interested in.

"Saki Ayase, huh?" he said. "Hmm…of all people, why her?"

"Oh, um, I don't know. She's quite good-looking, right?"

"Forget it."

"Huh?!"

"I'm saying this as your friend. I don't recommend her at all."

"Wait. What're you talking about?"

"I know it isn't cool to meddle in someone else's love life, but…"

"I don't recall talking to you about my love life."

I panicked, realizing Maru had assumed I was talking about a crush and was steamrolling ahead with that assumption.

"You weren't?" he asked. "I thought you'd fallen in love with Ayase."

"No way—I couldn't. A lousy guy like me would be a poor match for a pretty girl like her."

I envisioned the beautiful girl with her gorgeous blond hair, followed by my own dull face that had looked back at me from the mirror that morning. I sighed.

Maru eyed me suspiciously, like he wanted to ask what the heck I was talking about, and slowly shook his head.

"You've got it the wrong way around," he said. "It would be bad for your reputation if you started dating her."

"…Ha-ha. Are you trying to be funny?"

"I'm not joking."

"Then what are you saying? You must have a pretty inflated idea of how cool I am if you think I'm too good for her."

"She *is* a babe…but, well, I've heard a lot of bad rumors about her."

Talk about beating around the bush.

"I don't like saying things about people I don't know well," he continued, "but it's a different story if my best friend might be in love with her. They say ignorance is bliss, but knowledge is power."

"Will you tell me more about those rumors?"

Maru was still under the impression that I had the hots for Ayase, but if I corrected him, I'd have to explain that she was my stepsister. I didn't want the hassle of being interrogated, so I thought, what the heck? I'd just go along with it.

Maru looked around, then quietly moved closer. He spoke in a solemn, low voice.

"People say Ayase's...*selling.*"

"...Huh?"

"She dyes her hair blond, has pierced ears, and keeps people away with her sour look. She's a bad girl, an outcast at a prep school like ours, and she doesn't get along with her class. People have seen her leaving Shibuya's entertainment district and the area where all the cheap hotels are."

"Hmm. So that's what people are saying about her?"

I acknowledged what Maru had said, neither affirming nor denying it.

Unsurprisingly, her appearance made people think she was a stereotypical bad girl. From our few conversations, that wasn't my impression of her, but I didn't know her well enough to trust her unconditionally.

"Maru, it seems unusual for you to believe stuff like that. You're normally wary of rumors."

"A guy on the baseball team confessed to her."

"Huh? Aren't people scared of her?"

"They say bad things about her, but she's beautiful, and beautiful girls are popular. Though, I don't get it, personally."

"I see."

"But she told him—the guy who confessed, that is."

"...Told him what?"

"She said, 'I'm the bad girl everyone says I am, and I'm not interested in dating anyone.'"

Maru put on a high-pitched voice as if to mimic her. He was making light of the story, but it was clear he didn't have a good impression of Ayase.

"Any chance the guy might be exaggerating?"

"I can't be a hundred percent sure, but probably not. And he isn't the only one who's said things about her. I've heard similar stories from guys on other teams."

"Each story by itself leaves room for doubt, but put them all together, and they make for strong evidence, huh?"

"That's what I'm saying."

People didn't always tell the truth, but I thought it was very likely Maru was right about Ayase's responses to the boys who had confessed to her.

"Hmm... It's like Pandora...," I said.

I felt like I'd opened Pandora's box.

According to *The Chemistry of Men and Women*, you should first get to know the other person. I'd wanted to learn about Ayase to help me figure out how to interact with her, but now it seemed like I had even more to worry about.

Were the rumors true?

If so, did Akiko and Dad know?

And if they didn't, should I tell them about it now that we were a family?

...No.

I didn't like the idea of telling on someone without any proof or supporting evidence. And even if the rumors were true, I wasn't interested in meddling in someone else's affairs. So what if Ayase dated men for money? If they each had something the other wanted, they were free to do whatever they pleased. It was none of my business what she did.

Now that she was part of my family, things were a little more complicated, but I didn't want to criticize her, even if it was all true. My only thought was that it would be sad if there was something in her life that had driven her to do things like that.

"So, Asamura. Your turn."

"...What are you talking about?"

"I laid my cards on the table. Now you do the same. Why are you suddenly asking me about Ayase?"

"Oh. Well, you can think what you want."

"What? Don't brush me off—you're just making me curious."

"It's not that I won't tell. I can't say anything more. I wish you'd get the message."

"Hey, don't think you can distract me by quoting a line from a manga... Geez. Some friend you are. And after I told you what you wanted to know."

Maru complained under his breath, but he didn't push further. He knew when to quit. That was the good thing about Tomokazu Maru.

I glanced at the back of his head as he began preparing for first period; then I turned my attention to the window. I saw a reflection of myself leaning my cheek on my palm, looking bored as I thought absently about Ayase.

I was glad we weren't in the same class. If I was able to see her whenever I wanted, I'd never break free from this strange, anxious feeling.

I knew I'd feel it again when I got home, but it was human nature to want to delay the inevitable as much as possible.

The moment I'd wanted to delay came much sooner than expected—two hours later, to be precise.

Fate is merciless.

We had physical education class during third period every Monday, and the timing couldn't have been worse.

Sports Day was coming up, and classes paired up and had PE together to conduct practice games. These joint classes were beginning that very day.

"Okay, here goes! My secret weapon, the Great Soaring Serve! Take that!"

We were on the school tennis court, and under a blanket of thick, gray clouds, a carefree voice called out the names of fancy techniques, like the kind you might read about in manga.

The voice belonged to a female student in gym clothes, swinging away with her racket. She was petite, and her hair was dyed reddish-brown. She looked like a redheaded hamster moving restlessly around the court.

She was in a different class, but even I knew her name—Maaya Narasaka.

She was her class's representative. You might call her energetic if you were being nice. If you weren't, you might say she was loud and obnoxious.

She was cheerful to a fault, like she'd been doused with an energy drink, and a total mother-hen type. Maybe thanks to that and to her charming, cute face, she had friends throughout the school. She was living life to the fullest—an extrovert among extroverts.

Naturally, she also had a network of friends in my class and often came by to chat with them. That was why even a guy like me, who had nothing to do with school gossip, knew who she was.

Maaya Narasaka hit the ball into the sky, and it soared up as if sucked into the clouds. Her competitor, the spectators, and everyone else lost sight of it. They all held their breath as they awaited the moment when the ball would rip back through the clouds and strike like a missile.

One second... Two... Three...

"Hey, where the heck were you aiming? The ball's gone!" Maaya's opponent cried out after her amazing out-of-the-park home run.

"Ah-ha-ha! Sorry!"

"Geez. Why do you hit the ball so hard? You can't even control it."

"Because it's cool! Heh-heh!"

"'Heh-heh' my ass, you little show-off! Take this!"

"Aaahhh! Please, anything but a noogie!"

Maaya laughed as her opponent put her in a headlock and rubbed her knuckles into the other girl's head.

Cute girls playing around made for a pretty picture, and it had most of the guys in my class entranced, their eyes glued to the exchange.

But not me. I paid no attention to the lovely ladies. My eyes were focused elsewhere—on an individual leaning unobtrusively against the chain-link fence off in one corner of the court.

With no racket in hand, she was listening to something on her earphones, the cables coming out of her pocket, while she stared aimlessly at nothing.

It was Ayase.

She wasn't even trying to hide that she was skipping class. She stood clearly out in the open, blending into the scenery as if she belonged there. No one seemed to think her out of place, and neither the students nor the PE teacher appeared likely to reprimand her.

A bad girl who was an outcast in class and dated men for money. If a painting with a title like that existed, I was sure it would be a scene like this.

The other kids were chatting happily as they hit the ball back and forth. Meanwhile, I took advantage of my plain looks and the lack of attention they drew and quietly approached Ayase.

I leaned against the fence and sat down like I was resting in the shade.

"Skipping class?" I asked casually.

She removed her earphones and looked at me suspiciously. Then her eyes went wide.

"This is a surprise," she said. "Why are you talking to me?"

"I get curious when I see someone I know skipping class."

"Hmm. So you're here to lecture your younger sister?"

"No, nothing like that. I'm not such a good person that I can start lecturing other people. I just noticed that you also chose tennis for Sports Day."

"Maaya suggested we choose the same thing, though that isn't the only reason."

"Maaya Narasaka? Are you guys close?"

I glanced back toward the tennis court.

"Yeah," she said. "Though, I mean, I don't think there's a single girl at school who doesn't get along with her."

"So she really does have a hundred friends. Wow."

There were twenty girls per class, times eight, making it roughly a hundred and sixty in our grade. The number seemed astronomical.

"Maaya probably doesn't count them all as her real friends," she explained. "But she's bright and cheerful and can get along with anyone, even if they aren't close."

"Oh, that makes sense."

Ayase had me oddly convinced.

"So, Asamura, why did you choose tennis?"

"Um, do I have to say? It isn't anything impressive."

"That's okay. My other reason is that I'm pathetic."

What did she mean, "that's okay"? This wasn't some game where one embarrassing truth canceled out another.

She stared at me blankly, but her eyes implored me to go on, and eventually, I gave in and told her.

"In tennis, there aren't any team competitions."

Other sports, like basketball, soccer, and softball, which Maru had chosen, were team events. Tennis was the only sport without team or doubles competitions. The tournament would be singles only. This meant that if multiple students from a single class continued winning, they would eventually play one another.

"I chose tennis because I wanted to avoid team competitions."

If you're wondering why I would say that, you must be very lucky.

I didn't like expecting things from others or having others expect things from me. I would cringe at the mere thought of making a mistake and causing problems for my team. Anyone unbothered by troublesome thoughts like these must be about 80 percent better off than I was.

"Oh yeah...?" said Ayase. "We really do think alike."

Anyone who could relate to that feeling was more or less admitting to being an introvert.

"You're like that, too?" I asked.

"Well, yeah. I chose tennis because Maaya suggested it, but I didn't want to play team sports in the first place. I think you've started to notice, but I stay away from the other kids."

What she was saying was sad, but Ayase's tone was dry and without any hint of loneliness.

No one complained, even though she was clearly playing hooky and listening to music on her smartphone. It almost felt like she and her surroundings were stuck in a parallel world.

Wondering if she might be transparent, I squinted and looked at her, but her facial features were clear, and I could smell her fancy perfume. Her presence was too much, and I looked away, aware I was blushing.

"Do you, maybe, not really fit in with your class?" I asked.

"Is that a surprise?"

"Well, yeah. I thought stylish girls were the center of attention."

"That's generally true."

"But not me," she left unsaid.

People probably did say negative things about Ayase, though whether they were substantiated was anyone's guess. Still, most of the students believed the rumors.

"I'm in a pretty good position right now, though," she said. "...I couldn't care less about Sports Day. It sounds like a waste of time. And as long as people leave me alone, I can do whatever I want."

"Is that why you're listening to music?"

"Huh? ...Oh, well, yeah," she said evasively, averting her eyes.

She was hiding something, but it wouldn't be polite to intrude further. She'd talk when she felt like it, if it was something she could share with me. I'd be harassing her if I tried to dig it out before then, and I hated people who did that.

"This time, I'm going to get it right! My secret technique, the Ultra Soaring Serve!"

"That's not even the same name as before, lol!"

I could hear Maaya and her friend cavorting on the court again. They were really loud.

Just then, something occurred to me, and I looked at Ayase.

"Aren't you going to practice with Maaya? She must have suggested you choose tennis so she could play you."

"Nah."

"Wow, you didn't even need to think about it."

"I don't want to play tennis. Maaya knew I'd be sitting out when she made the suggestion... I guess that flexibility is another secret to her popularity."

As she said this, I felt some of Ayase's usual stiffness leave her voice.

The way she looked, the fact that she was playing hooky, the things she said—everything substantiated the rumors about her. But the personality I kept glimpsing within seemed to cancel out everything else.

I wondered who the real Saki Ayase was.

But I didn't know enough about her to figure out the answer.

When I arrived home from school, Akiko was just stepping out the door.

"Oh, Yuuta."

"Uh...I'm back."

"Welcome home! Dinner's ready!"

"Thank you...but you didn't have to do that. You're going to work, right?"

"I am," she said gently, placing one hand to her cheek. "Even though I've just moved, too. I can't get a break!"

She wore an expensive-looking top that elegantly exposed her shoulders, and her perfume was so intense that it made me dizzy. She radiated the sex appeal of an adult woman, like a butterfly sprinkling her charming scales wherever she went.

If she told me she was about to flutter off into the nighttime streets, it would sound like the most natural thing in the world.

"You don't have to go out of your way to make dinner for me," I said. "Dad's always busy, and I'm used to putting stuff together and eating alone."

"Most of my days with Saki were like that, too, but I don't know. We've just started living together, so I thought I should."

"Take it easy. I don't want you to work too hard and collapse."

"Okay. I might take you up on that starting tomorrow... Saki can cook, too, you know. Maybe the two of you can take turns."

My ears twitched at her casual words. I imagined Ayase cooking and instinctively felt it didn't suit her. And calling to mind the high school girl with blond hair and pierced ears reminded me of the bad rumors surrounding her.

A question arose in my mind, probably the result of those thoughts, and I asked it.

"By the way, where do you work?"

"In Shibuya's entertainment district."

"…What kind of business is it?"

"Oh, you think it's some sleazy place, don't you? Come on, now!"

Akiko puffed up her cheeks like a child, seeing through my attempt to dig into her background.

She was right. I couldn't bluff my way past a perceptive adult.

"It's a regular bar," she said. "We don't offer any improper services, and I only serve my customers from behind the counter."

"So you don't wait on them?"

"In a sense, I guess I do. I'm a bartender!"

She made a gesture like she was using a cocktail shaker. Even to my layman's eyes, her moves looked smooth and practiced. She didn't appear to be lying.

"I'm sorry I misunderstood. I thought…"

"You heard I worked late at night. I'm not surprised you assumed I was at some shady establishment. It's only natural. And besides, you're still a student. I'd prefer you *weren't* an expert in after-dark entertainment."

"I guess you have a point."

Thinking about it now, there was no way my dad could manage to seduce a woman who worked at a hostess bar. He was plain, ordinary, simple, and down-to-earth. He wasn't the type who could live it up amid the glittering nightlife. I should know; I'd been watching him for more than ten years—as far back as I could remember.

"Oops, I'd better be on my way," she said. "Take care of Saki, will you, Yuuta?"

"Oh, right! See you later."

Akiko waved good-bye and rushed down the stairway, like a butterfly soaring into the night.

…No, that wasn't right. She was more like a Chihuahua bounding through the grass in a park.

You could be so wrong about people when you judged them by their appearance or profession and relied on stereotypes.

After watching Akiko disappear past the elevator, I opened the front door...

I was inside our home, in my room.

This was supposed to be my haven, but I felt anxious, probably because the area beyond my door was now shared with strangers. The hallway, the living room, and the washroom—none of it belonged to my dad and me alone anymore.

It felt like a breach of etiquette to dwell on such things, so instead, I stared at the textbooks I'd put on my desk like I was trying to burn holes through them.

I studied for a while, then realized more than an hour had passed.

The sound of the front door opening and closing broke my concentration and brought me back to the real world. Moments later, I heard footsteps, then someone walking into the room next door.

"Welcome home," I said, but there was no reply. I must have spoken too softly for Ayase to hear through the wall between us.

I told myself that even if she had responded, I didn't have anything to talk about, and I turned back to my desk to resume my schoolwork.

I heard more footsteps through the wall, then the sound of her putting her schoolbag on the floor and opening her closet to pull clothes from a shelf...

Stop right there. It was gross of me to pay so much attention to the household noise from her room.

I overwrote my inner voice with the things in my textbook and waited for her presence to disappear.

"Asamura? Can I come in?"

But instead of disappearing, she knocked on my door and called out to me.

I took a second to glance around the room, judged what I saw acceptable, and responded:

"Uh...sure."

"Coming in!" she said back.

"Uh, so what did you need?"

"Oh, you're studying! Wow, it isn't even time for exams."

"I guess. I think this is normal, though."

It wasn't like I was always studying. I usually included manga and games in my daily routine as well. But my habit was to engage in those activities while in bed or sitting in the middle of my room like a slob. I could do that precisely because I knew no one was watching me, and I just couldn't get into the right mindset knowing that Ayase was on the other side of that thin wall.

"Are you aiming to get into a good college?" she asked.

"I don't think many people aim for a bad college."

"Seems like you're able to balance your schoolwork with your part-time job."

"Does that surprise you?"

It wasn't like the two were mutually exclusive.

"At a part-time job, you exchange your time for money," she explained. "But the more time you spend studying, the better you do in school. That's why I think it's tough to strike a balance."

"You're thinking too hard. I've never looked at it like that."

"Hmm... Oh, hey."

She averted her eyes and played around with the ends of her hair like she was about to say something difficult. Maybe it was just the lighting, but her cheeks looked slightly red.

You could tell she was intelligent even from our short exchange, and combined with the childlike way she kept changing expressions, I started wondering if the rumors at school about her sleeping around for money and being a delinquent were unfounded.

A few seconds passed, and Ayase's eyes took on a stern cast, like she was bracing herself to say what she wanted.

"Do you know of an easy part-time job that pays well and doesn't take up too much time?" she asked.

"So they *were* right."

"Huh?"

"Oh, nothing…"

I'd spoken on reflex.

I was glad I hadn't said something harder to gloss over. It would have been disastrous if I'd said something like, "So you *are* a prostitute."

"I want money but don't want to spend too much time working. It would be great if I could make more than a hundred dollars in an hour or two."

"A regular job won't pay that much," I said, pretending to be calm. I mentally put an iron mask over my face.

"Oh, okay. I guess *selling* is my only option."

I wished she wouldn't break through my protective gear so easily.

We might be only stepsiblings, but she *was* my sister. What on earth was she telling her new older brother?

"I read in a book that you have to sell yourself to make money," she said.

What kind of books was she reading? It'd be nice if people wouldn't leave suspicious books lying around where a high school kid could pick them up. Not that I was one to talk, considering the sleazy books I was pretty sure we sold in the comic-essay section.

"Um, Ayase. It might be a breach of etiquette to say what I'm about to say."

"It's fine, go ahead. I started it."

"I think you should take better care of yourself."

"Aren't you exaggerating? Other kids my age do it."

"Never mind other people. I'm talking about you. Only you can take care of yourself."

"I do take care of myself. That's why I want to build a nest egg."

Ayase had a surprisingly serious look in her eyes as I lectured her like some middle-aged man.

Dating for money, sugar daddies, anonymous hookups through social media—I'd thought girls who were into shady activities did those things without much thought. But Ayase looked so driven, I felt her gaze pull all those assumptions from my brain by the roots.

No matter what kind of resolve was behind her decisions, though, there were some things one shouldn't do. The fact that she was no longer a stranger, but my stepsister, only made me more determined.

I also felt guilty recalling the gentle look on Akiko's face when we ran into each other at the door. She must have complete faith in her daughter.

"Could you say what you just told me in front of your mom?" I asked.

"...Sure. It might even make her happy. She'd say, 'My, Saki, you've grown up.'"

"That's some way to raise a child."

"Isn't it the same in your family? Wasn't your dad happy when you did the same thing?"

"No way. I know Dad's a little hopeless, but he'd still be sad if his kid did something like that... Hey, how come you're talking like I already do it?"

"Huh? You went to work just yesterday...to your part-time job."

"...My part-time job?"

"Yeah, your part-time job."

There was an odd silence between us.

I didn't know when we'd started misunderstanding each other, and I wordlessly tried to trace back the dots I had connected to form the wrong line.

Ayase also seemed to have realized we weren't on the same page and narrowed her eyes.

"What did you think I was talking about?" she asked.

"I thought you were talking about expensive off-the-books escort services."

"...Huh?"

Her voice was cold. One of the coldest I'd ever heard.

"Oh, I get it. Because I said I needed to sell *myself*, right?"

"I'm sorry! I was just confused!"

We went over the misunderstanding, and by the time we had it all hashed out, we were both hungry and moved to the dining room.

We reheated the traditional dinner that Akiko had prepared and helped ourselves. The meal consisted of stir-fried vegetables, miso soup, and fried fish.

We had both taken a sip of soup when Ayase made an unhappy sound.

I'd really insulted her with the mix-up earlier. There was no room for excuses, and I folded my hands together and bowed in apology.

She sighed deeply.

"Stop that. I know people talk about me. But unfortunately, with the way I look, it's a common misconception. It's my own fault, too, for using the rumors to keep away people I don't want to deal with."

"Ayase..."

It didn't sound like she was simply putting on a brave face, but the fact she seemed so used to it only spoke to how bad it really was. I couldn't help but imagine the level of gossip and prejudice she'd been subject to.

But there was something I found strange.

Ayase seemed to objectively understand that people's misconceptions stemmed from her fashion choices. But if she knew that, I had to wonder why she still chose to dress the way she did.

She must have realized what I was thinking, because she stopped eating her vegetable stir-fry and spoke.

"I don't blame you for thinking I'm strange or for wondering why I still dress like this even though I know it causes me problems."

"Well...I guess I am a little curious."

"It's my armor."

"Huh?"

"No one enters a battlefield unarmed, right? For me, outfits like this are my armor for getting by in society."

She pointed a finger at one of her ears. A fancy earring sparkled at her fingertip, snugly fit into her pierced ear. This was the kind of thing only some young women, bad girls or not, would have the courage to try. It was a sort of junior high rite of passage, bound to divide opinion between the younger and older generations. She would have been a hero to her peers, while the adults admonished her.

As a girl grew up, the attitude toward getting one's ears pierced changed, and for some reason, it ceased to be a problem. The morality around it was baffling.

It was only a piece of metal, no more than a few millimeters in size. But boy, did it define girls in some complicated ways. When she showed it to me, I spoke without thinking.

"Your armor?" I said. "Does it give you extra defense points? Or maybe it lets you attack twice in one turn."

"*Pfft...* Hilarious."

She'd thought I was funny.

Those were just words I'd picked up from games and novels based on games, stored in the shallowest part of my brain. They had slipped out because I couldn't keep up with what she was saying.

"Well, you're half-right. The point is to boost both my attack and defense."

"Isn't that a little violent? Fantasy novels are one thing, but the real world is pretty peaceful."

"There are battles here, too. They just happen out of sight."

Ayase sounded like a storybook character trying to draw me into some conflict in a parallel world. A plain, ordinary guy like me, Yuuta Asamura, led into a world of bloody, supernatural battles...but of course, that wasn't what was happening. I had decent grades in Japanese class and could understand Ayase was just using a sophisticated rhetorical expression.

When we'd taken the plastic wrap off the vegetable stir-fry, I'd removed the note from Akiko and placed it on a corner of the table. It read, Saki and Yuuta, heat this and enjoy it together, and Ayase glanced over at it.

"Did you see Mom today?"

"Yeah. She was leaving when I came home."

"She looks pretty when she goes to work, right?"

"Oh, um, well. Yeah."

I knew I sounded evasive. I had no idea how to compliment a woman who had become my stepmother in front of her flesh and blood.

Ayase lowered her voice to a whisper and looked into my eyes. Her tone had changed, as if she was about to tell me a ghost story...

"But you know, she never went to college."

"Oh, I see," I said, unmoved. That was nothing out of the ordinary.

Ayase looked surprised.

"Doesn't that make you think of anything?" she asked.

"...No, it doesn't."

"Never went to college, pretty, works in a bar. What do you get when you combine those three elements together?"

"A woman who never went to college, is pretty, and works in a bar, I guess?"

What the heck was she talking about? Sure, I had certain images in my head related to each of those things, but just combining them didn't add anything new to the mix.

"Hmm. You're so neutral, Asamura," she muttered before taking a bite of her vegetables.

Was it the pitiful delusions of a virgin that made me sense a whiff of pleasure hidden behind her relaxed expression? I wasn't familiar enough with the way girls thought to be sure I was wrong, which was frustrating.

"I think that's a great way to be," she said.

"I'm lucky you're so considerate of virgins like me."

You didn't have to be a mind reader to communicate effectively; you just had to be honest about what you were thinking.

But Ayase's gaze clouded over in an instant. I felt a chill down my spine. The "virgin" comment had been too much, I realized. But it didn't seem like she intended to call me out for my off-color remark. Instead, she spoke in an even more serious tone.

"I know what people think—people who aren't neutral. They see a pretty girl who never went to college working in a bar and think she's a stupid woman who uses her appearance as a weapon to make shady money. I've seen people look down on Mom like that many times."

"That's nonsense."

True, there might be some general correlation between one's education and intellectual abilities. But it was far from an absolute means of measuring an individual's capability. Maybe that kind of thing was accurate on a macro scale, but there were bound to be exceptions when one looked at specific cases. There was a big difference between saying, "Yeah, people are often like that," and "So she must be like that, too." Anyone who couldn't understand something so simple must be stupid, indeed.

...Or so a book Yomiuri once loaned me had said. It was amazing how much impact a book could have on you. Of course, I was only a high school kid, and I wasn't about to pretend to know all about life, but I got carried away and reflexively parroted the values of some book I'd read.

When she heard those borrowed words, however, Ayase's face flushed a little. She leaned forward and replied with gusto.

"Right? Total nonsense!"

"Y-yeah."

"And people like that are really underhanded, too. They use logic to back you into a corner."

"How so?"

"A smart woman who doesn't look good is called a despicable snob. Someone with a nice appearance and no brains got wherever she is by sleeping around. If a beautiful woman relies on a man, she's told she has it easy because she can sponge off some guy. But if she tries hard to make it on her own, she's pitiful because she can't find a man to take care of her."

"Oh...I see. Yeah, people do say those things."

"I bet boys have stuff like that, too."

"Oh yeah. When you try to promote yourself to a girl you like, you're called gross or a criminal or you're accused of sexual harassment. But when you turn around and say to heck with relationships, people say you're just sulking, trying to act tough, or feeling inferior because you're a virgin."

"Those are some really specific examples. Is that based on real-life experience?"

"You see stories like that on social media and stuff. Maybe because I heard about those experiences first, I decided I didn't want the same thing to happen to me. It sounds like a big hassle. So I made it a rule not to get involved in relationships."

"I see. Yeah, I get what you're saying."

She could have teased me by quoting Aesop's famous fable about sour grapes, but she simply agreed. The stiffness in her voice and expressions eased slightly. Maybe she could relate to something I'd said.

"So anyway, that's why my clothes are my armor."

And just like that, we were back on the topic of her clothes.

"I have to dress well and get to the point where others say I'm beautiful. Then I have to do flawlessly in school and at work. Dressing well is the first step to becoming a perfect, strong woman who can crush any fool who tries to put me in a box."

Her tone was matter-of-fact, as usual, but powerful emotion was seeping into her voice.

...She was my opposite.

I didn't want to deal with the roles people pushed on me, and I tended to stay away from others and run from my problems. Ayase, however, was the type who spat at the rest of the world and went on the offensive. She was strong.

But within that strength, I sensed a hint of fragility.

"Are you okay with that?" I asked. "Doesn't it tire you out?"

"As long as I prove them wrong, it's worth it to me."

*Prove who wrong?*

The question flitted through my mind, but it seemed awkward and nosy to ask, so I kept it to myself.

Her values seemed too old-fashioned for someone our age. Maybe they'd come from her real father—Akiko's ex-husband. In that case, I didn't want to trespass into her personal space. I didn't like it when people got nosy about my mom, so it was only right that I afforded others the same consideration.

I forgot what I wanted to say to her as thoughts like that whirled around in my mind. Then Ayase broke the silence.

"Aren't you the same?"

"I'm not strong like you, and I don't intend to fight against how others see me."

"But deep down, you think expectations are a hassle, right? Both the expectations others have of you and the idea of expecting things from other people."

She was right. That was why it'd been so easy for us to come to an agreement when we first met at the restaurant.

"We need the strength to live independently to free ourselves from the annoying expectations and judgments of other people," she said.

"I see. *That's* why you're looking for a well-paying part-time job."

"Oh-ho. You've seen right through me."

"You've been giving me so many hints. It was pretty obvious."

Ayase seemed impressed, but I just sagged my shoulders and continued: "You need the money to be independent, right?"

"Exactly... Sorry."

Ayase looked down awkwardly.

I didn't ask why she was apologizing. There was no need for me to quiz her on why she, someone who had probably never worked before, had started looking for a high-paying job so soon after joining the Asamura family. The answer was obvious.

She wanted to be strong and proud and live independently without depending on or expecting things from others, and now she was staying with new people who she could easily rely on.

"There's no simple way to make good money working part-time," I told her. "The wages I earn at the bookstore are pretty low, too."

"I see..." Ayase hung her head. "Then I guess I have no choice but to give up."

"You're not going to look into it yourself?"

"If I really take it seriously and start gathering information from scratch, I'll lose study time. I have zero information, since I've never had a job. I might be able to figure something out if I dedicate a lot of time to it, but it's not worth the effort. I'd end up having to choose between researching jobs and keeping my grades up, since I'm not smart enough to manage both."

"Okay, I see. I might have an easier time doing the research, since I have work experience and my network is bigger."

I didn't have that many friends myself, but according to what she'd just said, Ayase was a total loner. She seemed to be friends with Maaya, but I hadn't seen anyone else around her.

"I might be able to help you find the kind of job you're looking for," I said.

"Really?"

"Yeah. I have a friend at school who's pretty well-informed."

He was the only friend I had.

"And I have a coworker who's into all sorts of things. I think she might have some suggestions. I have a shift tomorrow, so I'll ask her then."

"Thanks. It isn't fair to keep asking you to do things for me, though, is it?"

She took a sip of her miso soup as she thought this over.

"Miso soup," I said.

"Huh?"

"I'd like you to make miso soup for me every day."

I was sitting at the dining table with a girl my age I'd only just met, like it was no big deal. As I took in this extraordinary scene, those words simply spilled out of me.

Ayase looked blank for a few seconds, her miso soup bowl still at her lips as if glued there.

"Was that a love confession?"

"No, no. That's not what I meant."

I wasn't surprised she'd thought that. Without any context, what I'd said was basically a Japanese-style marriage proposal.

I'd actually been thinking about Akiko saying it would be tough for her to cook dinner every day. If Ayase and I took turns, I'd have to cook. When it was just Dad and me, we'd make do with takeout, deliveries, instant-meal packs, and convenience-store fare, but that wasn't going to cut it anymore.

However, I had my job to think about, and I wanted time to study and to read books and manga. Even if we took turns, would I really be able to fit in cooking?

It had been years since I'd last had homemade miso soup, but I knew it tasted much better than instant.

These thoughts had been swirling in my brain for a while, and they were the reason I'd blurted out that line about miso soup.

"Well, okay," she said. "I don't particularly mind cooking. I'm pretty good at it, too, so it won't take up all my time like researching jobs would."

It appeared I'd managed to convince her.

"Then I'll provide you with information on lucrative job opportunities…," I said.

"And I'll make meals for you," said Ayase.

Although we knew it was bad manners, we pointed at each other's faces and confirmed that we had ourselves a deal.

# ● JUNE 9 (TUESDAY)

Morning came, bringing with it no dramatic events, such as a personal wake-up call from my stepsister.

The night before, Ayase had bathed last again and gone to bed after I fell asleep. She must have gotten up before me as well and was now preparing herself for the day.

"Yuuta! You aren't going to believe this!"

I stepped out into the hall and ran into a clown with a face full of shaving cream. Correction: It was Dad getting ready for work. He opened his bloodshot eyes wide and flapped his lips as he pointed toward the living room.

"What are you so excited about?" I asked.

"I had just started shaving—"

"I can see that."

"—when I heard a noise from the kitchen and went to look."

"And?"

I wanted to tease him for making this sound like the setup to a murder reveal, but I held it in. Then he struck a pose like a dictator making a speech and said excitedly:

"It's S-Saki… She's making breakfast!"

"Is that so shocking?"

"Of course it is! Who would have thought the day would come when I would eat breakfast prepared by my own daughter?"

His glasses couldn't hide the tears of joy pooling in his eyes. It was great that he was so moved, but I wished he'd stop dripping shaving cream all over the floor.

"Okay… Well, why don't you go back to the bathroom and finish washing up?"

"That's cold, Yuuta. It wouldn't hurt for you to be a little more charming, like Saki."

"Ayase, charming?"

I thought of her cool bad-girl look and cocked my head in confusion. Sure, she had a cute face. She was definitely attractive. But *charming*? I had my doubts about how well that particular descriptor fit her.

…Mean thoughts swirled around my head as I pushed Dad into the bathroom and headed for the living area. There, I noticed the fragrant aroma of pepper wafting through the air.

"Are those eggs sunny-side up?" I asked Ayase.

"I know it's standard, but if you wouldn't mind, I'd like to keep it basic in the morning."

"I don't have any complaints, but can I say something?"

"That really sounds like the lead-up to a complaint…but go ahead."

"Why are you making breakfast?"

She hadn't made breakfast the previous day. Something like toast for breakfast was fine for Dad and me, and we were more than capable of making our own.

"We made a deal," she said. "Remember?"

"You mean what we talked about last night? Wasn't that about dinner?"

"Yeah, but I thought I might as well make breakfast while I was at it. My policy is to give a lot when I give and take."

"I see…"

Her response was beyond conscientious, and yet she delivered it in her usual matter-of-fact tone.

Ayase was wearing an apron over her school uniform. Seeing one's younger sister making a home-cooked meal first thing in the morning was a sight that would have a lot of guys salivating. But at the same time, Ayase was far from the kind of imaginary stepsister those guys fantasized about.

Feeling guilty that she was doing all the work, I considered what I could help with and decided to wipe the tabletop. She glanced at me from the kitchen and saw the shiny surface of the table reflecting the light.

"Thanks," she said awkwardly as she brought three plates of eggs into the dining area. How typical of her to thank me for something that any family member would do.

Next, she brought out the steamed rice and miso soup. Both were freshly made, fragrant, and piping hot.

"When did you whip these up?"

"I got the preparations done before bed last night—it wasn't much trouble."

She spoke casually, as if to stress that it wasn't a big deal. This was quite impressive to me, who had considered it too much trouble to bother for years.

We sat facing each other, folded our hands in front of our faces, and said our thanks for the meal just as Dad arrived, finally ready for work.

His eyes sparkled as he took in the standard Japanese breakfast on the table.

"This is so moving…"

"Ah-ha-ha. You're exaggerating, Dad," Ayase said, smiling wryly.

Her attitude toward him was different from the cool, dry tone she used with me. I figured it was her way of showing respect for the new adult in her life.

Judging by the emotional distance and the subject matter of their conversation, Ayase seemed less like a stepsister and more like a bride who had just married into our family.

Dad devoured the eggs, commenting all the while on how delicious they were, then said it was time to go and quickly took off for work.

I was appalled by how quickly he'd finished eating. That said, I'm usually a fast eater, too. But this morning, I had a reason to slow down.

"Don't you like your breakfast?" Ayase asked.

She looked at me with worry as I continued eating slowly and silently, not explaining myself.

"That's not it," I said.

"You don't have to be polite. If it doesn't suit your taste, I'll make something different next time."

"No, I mean it."

She had stuck to the basics, preparing the eggs by the book without any weird special touches. The yolk and the overall shape were a perfect circle and tasted as good as they looked. Whereas little sisters in manga and anime tended to be ludicrously bad at cooking, Ayase was cool, subdued, and competent.

So why wasn't I gobbling down her cooking?

"It's just that I often pour soy sauce on my fried eggs...," I said awkwardly. "So I'm not used to eating them like this."

I was being honest. That was my only reason.

Ayase had used salt and pepper. Unfortunately, she hadn't cooked the eggs in a way that left room for other seasonings. I wasn't allergic to salt and pepper and could eat the eggs just fine, but soy sauce added moisture, so they were dry compared with what I was used to, and the sensation on my tongue and throat as they went down felt wrong.

"Fried eggs with soy sauce... I didn't know a combination like that existed...," Ayase muttered, sounding surprised. From my standpoint, however, it was more shocking to eat eggs with only salt and pepper.

Ayase's expression didn't change much, but she lowered her shoulders slightly as she spoke.

"Sorry. I cooked the eggs how I like them and didn't think about what you might want."

"Oh, please, it's nothing for you to be sorry about. It's my fault for not mentioning it and worrying you by eating so slowly."

"From now on, I'll try to ask about your preferences beforehand."

"Okay. I'll make sure I tell you stuff, too."

And that was that. We talked it out and reached a compromise. *This is kind of nice*, I thought. Our exchange might have sounded cold and matter-of-fact to someone else, but it was a relief for me.

After spending some time together that morning, Ayase and I once again

left for school at different times. This was both to ensure that our class-mates didn't grow suspicious of us and to help maintain a healthy distance between ourselves.

Ayase was family, but she was also a girl, and we were the same age. I felt bad enough that she had to worry about how to act around me at home. Trying to maintain the right distance in public would just make it harder on both of us.

I wanted to cherish my time alone, and so did she. Keeping that up would be key to maintaining a good relationship in the future.

"Which do you like better, cryptocurrency or becoming a YouTuber?"

"Forget both for now."

Maru and I were lazily waiting for morning homeroom to begin. As soon as he arrived, I'd hit him with a choice, and he'd ruthlessly rejected both options in less than a second.

"I'm impressed by how quickly you make decisions," I said. "I guess that's why you're the regular catcher."

"Anyone would say the same thing. What's gotten into you all of a sudden?"

"I'm looking for a way to make money quickly and efficiently."

I chose my words carefully. I couldn't break my promise with Ayase and tell him about our conversation, so this was as much as I could say. Naturally, he wasn't satisfied and eyed me suspiciously.

"Asamura...don't tell me some scam artist is trying to rip you off or something."

I wanted to joke that Ayase was filling me up (with delicious breakfast), not ripping me off, but I held it in. I was a man of my word.

"I haven't turned to crime or anything," I said, "but it's hard to find stability these days, even if you start working for a big company. And a career as a public servant sounds pretty hard. It can't hurt to start building a savings account, right?"

"That sounds like a decent life plan."

"For starters, I'd like to take paid dating off my list."

"I'm surprised it was there in the first place, but… Hmm." I could see a glint of suspicion from behind Maru's glasses. "You asked me about Saki Ayase yesterday, and now you're looking for a shady part-time job. Don't tell me you're—"

"N-no, I'm not."

I was quick to deny what he was about to say. I knew he'd only be more suspicious, since I hadn't even let him finish, but I couldn't help it.

He swallowed and stared into my eyes as I waited for him to say something. He carefully searched my expression, then dived straight to the point.

"Forget it, Asamura. You can try to sell your body, but you won't find any customers. Just take a look in the mirror."

"…*Haah.*"

I sighed in relief. The energy drained from me so quickly that I couldn't even bring myself to object to Maru's insult.

*Thanks, Maru, for being weirdly dense.*

"You just thought something rude about me, didn't you?" he said.

"No, I didn't," I lied casually.

It wasn't really a lie anyway. I wasn't being rude—only silently thanking him.

As it turned out, stereotypes were a force to be reckoned with. Behind his glasses, my best friend was the regular catcher for our school's baseball team and a terrific student with excellent insight and powers of observation. Yet even *he* couldn't bring himself to associate Ayase with the words *younger sister.*

The image people had of her was that of a bad girl suspected of dating for money, not a *sister*; this was simply more proof of how hard it was for people to combine those conflicting ideas.

"Anyway," Maru said, sticking out his index finger like a wife telling her husband what was what, "for starters, you're underestimating the world if you think you can make quick, easy money as a YouTuber or with cryptocurrency."

"Y-you think?"

"Yeah, you are. Successful people are serious about what they do and spend more time at it than you can imagine. It's like baseball. You aren't going to hit a home run merely by swinging the bat and hoping you'll get lucky."

"Oh, I see. When you put it that way, it makes sense."

Maru had sunk a lot of time into baseball, and that made his argument especially convincing. But while I could see his point, I sensed a shadow of contradiction in his words.

"Though, you know," I said, "some people only start making decent money after a decade of work, while others make a huge fortune in a year. I wonder what the difference is. I can't believe it's only a matter of how much time they put into it."

"I don't know. It isn't like I'm making money myself. Maybe there's a trick to doing things right."

"A trick, huh…?"

"Maybe it's about attitude. My folks are into history, and they raised me talking about stuff like the Warring States period and *Romance of the Three Kingdoms*, so I have all this knowledge about battle tactics…"

"Yeah. You do remind me of Zhuge Liang sometimes."

You start to get a sense of how a person talks when you've been chatting with him for more than a year, and Tomokazu Maru was quite the strategist.

At the previous year's Sports Day, he'd collected information on the other classes from who knows where and passed it on to the people competing in our class. As a result, we did great in most of the events.

Maybe it was those qualities that had helped score Maru his position on the baseball team.

"I don't know if I'd go that far…," he said, "but I guess the basic concepts of war got imprinted in my brain."

"What concepts are those?"

"Information and knowledge are the greatest weapons you can have."

"Like 'know your enemy, know yourself, and you shall not fear a hundred battles'?"

"Exactly. The number of enemy soldiers, the locations of their bases, the number of weapons they have, what their plans are—information like that is crucial. And there's no way a guy with a stone ax could ever defeat an enemy with the technology to shoot at long range from unmanned aircraft."

"Okay, so if we apply those concepts to making money...what are we lacking? Knowledge?"

"I think so. I bet you'd have a lot more success if you understood the mechanisms of society and how people do business—not that I do or anything."

Maru sounded like he knew what he was talking about, but he adopted a devil-may-care attitude in the end. I supposed it was a show of his sincerity to avoid sounding sure when he wasn't, even when he was just giving advice to a friend.

But I felt what he was saying was right. I knew my best friend was a guy I could depend on. I mentally noted down the approaches he'd suggested.

Once school was out, I hopped on my bicycle and headed straight for the bookstore where I worked.

Our store was located right by Shibuya Station, and while many young people came to browse our books, we also saw a lot of office workers and people from the entertainment district during the week as well. Thanks to the recent laws restricting overtime, our peak hours were usually between six and eight PM. After that, however, things calmed back down, and the number of workers decreased to around four for the late shift.

Two staff members took breaks at eight, and I was left alone with Yomi-uri for about an hour. She stifled a yawn at the cash register as I pretended to put things in order on the sales floor and wandered around the aisles searching for books.

First, I needed information about money, and it had to be accurate.

I picked up a few titles that looked reasonably simple on topics such as economics, business, and the structure of capitalism. Their titles and tag-lines looked similar, and it was hard to tell how they differed, but I chose the ones that seemed most credible based on their author bios and tables of contents.

I also picked up several magazines with high-paying want ads. I could have checked for similar information online using my phone, but I wanted to avoid any shady deals.

Of course, just because a classified ad was placed in a reputable magazine didn't guarantee that it was legitimate. I was pretty sure all it did was make me feel better, but that was something.

…Okay.

I'd gathered a pile of books and magazines that seemed to have the information I was looking for and was heading to the cash register when someone poked me in the shoulder.

"Hey, you shouldn't be browsing books for yourself while you're on the clock."

It was Yomiuri.

"Oh, sorry," I said.

"Just kidding. It's no problem. No one follows rules like that. Even the manager sets aside books for himself while he's working. As long as you use common sense and aren't unfairly hogging new releases that everyone wants or works by popular authors that sell out, it should be fine."

Yomiuri slapped me on the shoulder and laughed merrily.

Compared with what you might expect from her graceful, quiet, bookish appearance, Yomiuri was an easygoing, lighthearted person. She once told me she'd been popular with the guys when she started college, but that popularity had dwindled when she went out drinking and they caught a glimpse of her true nature. She said she wished people wouldn't take for granted that she was pure and innocent.

*"I can't help it if my dark hair and face make me look meek. I was just born this way."*

I can still remember her sulky expression as she played around with the tips of her hair. Most guys clearly expected all flirty girls to dye their hair and wear heavy makeup, and I could understand why she didn't like the social pressure to dress a certain way.

Now that Ayase, a girl who was Yomiuri's opposite in a sense, had become my stepsister, I could understand her feelings even better. Humanity really needed to give up on stereotypes.

"So, Yuuta. What are you buying?"

"Please don't look."

"That's some reaction! Don't tell me it's porn."

"That's way too bold for a guy like me with a brand-new stepsister... and I'm too young to buy X-rated books anyway."

"Then let me see them... Gotcha!"

"Oh crap!"

She'd grabbed the pile of books from me at lightning speed.

"Hmm. Hmm... Hmm?"

As Yomiuri looked at the covers one by one, a strange expression appeared on her face.

"I didn't know you were so serious about your future," she said. "Out to make a lot of money?"

"Y-you've got it all wrong," I said immediately, afraid she'd start teasing me.

I didn't think it would be right to share anything about Ayase, so I decided to leave her name out of my explanation.

"I want to move out and get my own place as soon as I graduate high school, so I need to start saving money."

"Isn't one part-time job enough?"

Her opinion was perfectly valid.

"Well, um, no. I work here because I love books, but the pay isn't all that great."

"Oh. I guess you have a point."

"I have a stepsister now, and I've started feeling like I can't just stick around. I don't want to be a burden on her."

"Oh, really?"

Yomiuri's tone and expression remained unchanged, but her response sounded skeptical.

"You aren't convinced?" I asked.

"I understand why you'd want to move out, but I don't believe you about your sister being the reason," she said seriously.

I froze. I'd simply been relating Ayase's argument as if it was my own, and I was caught unawares.

"Isn't it simply a matter of how I feel?" I asked.

"I wasn't denying your feelings. I just think they're unreasonable."

"You don't think my reasoning is valid?"

"It just seems like a waste."

"Huh?"

I blinked. I hadn't expected her to say something like that.

"You said you don't want to be a burden," she said, "...but if that's really how you feel, I don't think you'll be able to make a lot of money, no matter how many of these books you read."

"You've lost me. Can you take me through that again, step by step?"

"Having a sister your age is actually an asset. And living without depending on others is like trying to do things with your hands and feet tied."

She spoke bluntly, but her words were strangely piercing.

Ayase was the one who wanted to live without depending on Dad or me, but since I'd sympathized with her, Yomiuri's words really hit me.

"Yuuta, why do you think we need money?" she asked.

"Well, we need it to live."

"You think so?"

"Is this a Zen question? All right, then. We need money for food, shelter, and clothes."

That was how capitalism worked.

"Hmm, okay. Then to take an extreme example, will a baby die if it can't make money?"

"That *is* extreme."

"Babies survive, even without working for a living."

"They still need parental protection, though."

"Right. They have help... Can't the same thing be true for adults?"

"Whoa. No, of course not."

Society would collapse if everyone started asking for help. Society functioned because adults protected their children, made money, and supported themselves.

"But these days, more and more people want to be babies," Yomiuri pointed out.

"Isn't that judging society based on only a small group?" I countered.

It was true that I'd seen posts here and there on social media with people treating cartoon characters like their mothers or transparently wishing they could go back to being a baby. Still, not all adults were like that...or so I hoped. Could I be wrong?

"I'm not saying it's universal, of course," she said, "but when you see posts like that going viral, you have to assume a fair number of people feel the same way."

"Well...I guess you have a point."

"We all start out as babies. But once we're adults, we're suddenly pushed away and told we have to start acting differently. Isn't that cruel?"

"...I suppose so."

"This is another extreme example, but as long as someone provides us with food, clothes, and a place to live, we can still survive even without money, right?"

"Like a kind of nonmonetary basic income?"

"Wow! You're a real man of the world."

"Stop it."

I wished Yomiuri wouldn't treat me like a kid dying to use a fancy phrase he'd just learned.

That phrase, by the way—*basic income*—referred to a government regularly distributing a certain amount of money to its citizens. I'd read about it in a book that Yomiuri had suggested to me. There was really no need for her to tease me about it.

She laughed it off and told me not to worry so much.

"I think it's okay to depend on someone if you can't survive alone," she said.

"Even if you're a burden to them?"

"Some people say they like those kinds of women."

"Everyone has their own preferences."

"I suppose you aren't like that."

"...I don't know."

I figured it was fair to say that Ayase wouldn't want that sort of man, at least...not that I really knew her, of course. That was why I decided to simply say I didn't know.

"But hey, that's how money really works," said Yomiuri. "It's great if you have it; if you don't, you can get someone to help you. And you should help others whenever you can so they'll give you a hand when you're in trouble. That kind of thinking will get you closer to becoming rich than reading books like these."

"You think so?"

"I know so. Few CEOs are more skilled than those working under them."

"That's a bold statement."

"It's true. CEOs are much more talented at getting people to help them than you might imagine, young one."

"It isn't cool to be a smart-ass."

"What? You don't think a lovely college girl like me would have a rich sugar daddy or two?"

"What?!"

I froze. *Sugar daddy*. This impure, suggestive phrase twisted around in my mind.

Was she talking about that recent phenomenon where a girl lived off an older man? Or had my ears made a vulgar mistake, and she'd only been talking about her own father? If that was the case, it seemed strange for her to have two, but if her parents had remarried like mine, it was possible she had two dads.

On the other hand, if I'd heard correctly, that would be quite the shock. It wasn't as if I had a crush on her, and having worked with her, I knew she wasn't an innocent maiden as her appearance might suggest.

Still, I couldn't help being surprised. I'd had the same reaction when

I heard the rumors about Ayase selling herself. It seemed I was weak to subjects like these. Maybe, as a virgin, I was doomed to feel this way.

I stood there anxiously brooding for a few seconds, when I saw a devilish grin cross Yomiuri's face like she had just pulled one over on me.

"Just kidding!"

"Hey, get outta here!" I cried.

I dropped all pretense of formality. But could you blame me?

"I have a college friend who has one, though, so I hear stories," she said. "It sounds like rich people are generally good at depending on others. And just in case you're not convinced, that friend has a new brand-name item every week."

"Wow."

I felt like I'd gotten a glimpse at the dark side of college life, but it was a relief that Yomiuri hadn't been talking about herself.

"Well, anyway, why don't you try relying on your parents before you turn to advice from books like these?" she said.

With a wink, she went to help a customer who'd just approached the register. I watched her serve them with that sweet, innocent smile, then eyed the worldly titles of the books in my arms.

In the end, I left the bookstore that day without buying any of them.

"Hi, Ayase. I'm home."

"Welcome back, Asamura."

When I got home, I was met by my stepsister, cool as a cucumber, and the stimulating aroma of spices tickling my nostrils.

I walked into the living room and saw Ayase working in the kitchen. I couldn't be sure if she'd just returned from school or simply hadn't changed out of her uniform, but she had an apron over it as she stirred a huge pot with a ladle.

"Hope work went well. Do you want to eat right away?"

"Thanks. I'll get the plates."

"Oh, that's okay. You must be tired," Ayase said as I grabbed a few plates from the cupboard.

I smiled wryly to myself. This exchange made us sound more like a new-lywed couple than brother and sister. But no way was I going to say that.

After working together (not that I did much), Ayase and I finished preparing for dinner, sat across from each other, and began eating.

That evening, we were having curry. It had plenty of chunky vegetables and looked good for your health. There was even a side salad. It was scary how much care Ayase had put into the meal.

When I put a spoonful of the fine mix of vegetables and spices into my mouth, my eyes went wide.

"It's delicious...!" I said, unable to keep in my honest praise.

"I'm glad," Ayase replied.

The curry was so good that I didn't have to waste any time thinking up a compliment. This wasn't one of those all-in-one boxes of curry powder you bought at the supermarket, where you simply followed the instructions.

The delicate texture wouldn't have been possible if Ayase hadn't used several spices and calculated how long she had to simmer the vegetables. The rice wasn't sticky, either, so she must have cooked it in some special way. I was surprised by how quickly I was shoveling it down.

Ayase's reply was curt, but it was clear my comment had pleased her. I could swear I saw the corner of her mouth turn up slightly as she ate.

Her brow furrowed a little as the spices hit her tongue, causing her to drop her cool facade for a moment and reminding me she was just as human as the rest of us.

"I didn't expect you to make such an authentic curry," I said.

"I'd give myself a score of around seventy out of a hundred."

"Are you saying you could have done better?"

"I didn't have time to marinate the meat, so I cut a few corners. Sorry."

"Marinate the meat?"

Like a parrot, I repeated the unfamiliar words.

"You're kidding," she said. "Do I have to tell you what that means?"

"I know nothing about cooking... Though, I do know you cook both sides of a steak."

I probably sounded like someone from a parallel universe to her.

"Well, whatever," she said before launching into an explanation. "When you cook meat straight from the pack, it isn't that good, and it can be a little stinky. Adding salt and pepper, and maybe garlic and some other spices, then letting it soak them up helps the flavor. You don't have to use as much salt afterward, so it can also help you save on ingredients."

"Wow... That's some wisdom for everyday life."

"It's just something I read online. I get most of my information from recipe sites."

According to Ayase, no one had shown her how to cook—she was self-taught. I began to realize that her desire to be independent wasn't just a passing idea.

Still unsure what to say exactly, I decided to broach the subject with her.

"So about making quick money."

"Oh yeah. You looked into it for me?"

"I did, but I don't have anything for you yet. Even though you made a tasty meal in exchange. I'm sorry."

"...I see. Well, it isn't easy."

Her shoulders drooped, but she didn't look as disappointed as I'd thought she'd be. Knowing Ayase, she'd probably given it a shot herself before coming to me for help. She must have already known how hard it was to find a part-time job that was safe and paid well.

"But I did hear about what characteristics can make a person rich," I offered.

"Huh. That sounds interesting."

"Personally, I thought it made sense when I heard it."

I proceeded to tell Ayase what Yomiuri had said about the importance of cleverly depending on others. A curious look appeared in her eyes when I finished.

"So, Asamura, there *is* a girl you're close to."

"Huh?! That's your takeaway from what I said?"

"Oh, sorry. I just didn't expect it."

"Are you making fun of me, by any chance?"

"I said I'm sorry."

She flashed an apologetic smile. I didn't want her treating me like a virgin. Though, it was true that I'd never had intimate contact with a female to date, so she wasn't exactly wrong.

"I just kind of assumed you hated women," she said.

"That's not true. Why did you think that?"

"Your situation is similar to mine, so I figured we were alike."

*Oh, so you don't like girls?* I thought but kept that silly comment to myself.

By "situation," I figured she meant growing up with parents who didn't get along. She probably didn't have positive feelings about her biological dad and must have figured I was the same.

She was half-right.

It was true that I didn't get along with my biological mom.

"But those aren't the same thing," I said. "Just because I don't get along with one particular woman doesn't mean I hate all women."

"I see. That's a great attitude."

She sounded impressed. It didn't seem like she wanted to continue on this subject, however, and she casually brushed it off.

"Anyway," she said, "I'm rooting for you."

"...What about?"

"She's a kind older woman who loves books and has a nice figure, right?"

"Yeah, so?"

"I think you guys would make a cute couple."

"What?"

She smiled teasingly, and I frowned. It was true that Yomiuri was older than me, good-looking, and had big boobs, but she was also hard to read, and you had to stay on guard around her. She liked to establish dominance through teasing, which was okay when you had the room to deal with it but a little taxing when you were tired.

"Why do you look so unhappy?" Ayase asked. "I thought she gave good advice. And she seems like a nice, smart person."

"Well, I won't disagree with that," I said vaguely before clamming up.

I felt it would be really rude to tell another girl my honest opinion about Yomiuri, which was that she was too exhausting to date.

"But how disappointing," Ayase muttered, setting down her spoon. "What your coworker said is right, but I still want to be independent."

"You seem to be in an awful rush. Do you think Dad and I aren't reliable?"

"It's not that. You and your dad are nice, and you seem like people I can count on," she said. "It's just… I think it would have been a little easier if the two of you weren't such good people."

"What's that supposed to mean…?"

"Sorry. I know there's nothing you can say to that… I think I've had enough curry."

She looked surprised at her own words, as if she hadn't meant to say them. She quickly began clearing her dishes, though a little curry remained in her bowl.

I almost called out to her as she rushed into the kitchen, but I changed my mind. It had only been a few days since we became stepsiblings, but despite my limited experience with girls, even I could tell she didn't want to talk anymore.

I would probably go to bed with this awkward feeling still plaguing me. Bracing myself, I swallowed down the rest of the curry in my bowl.

It was very good, but the spice wasn't enough to cleanse the murkiness from my mind.

"I wonder if I'll be able to sleep okay…"

…In the end, I had no problem falling asleep that night.

That was because Ayase made a rare visit to my room to bring me something.

"What's this?" I asked.

"It's an aroma candle and a sleep mask. I'd feel bad if you couldn't sleep because I said something weird."

I couldn't believe how thoughtful she was.

She might be clumsy and a little cold, but she was obviously a very considerate person. This gesture added yet another layer of humanity to her in my mind.

# ● JUNE 10 (WEDNESDAY)

When you think back on the day's happenings, like when writing a diary, you seldom recall the scenes on your way to school in the morning. That's because memories of boring, routine activities are automatically deleted from your mind.

On the other hand, when something happens that makes a powerful impact or is simply worth mentioning, you will often start your description like this:

*It happened on my way to school…*

Well, today was just such a day.

I had two methods of getting to Suisei High. I either walked or rode my bicycle. It wasn't so far as to make walking impossible, but going on my bike was faster and easier.

That wasn't always the case, however. If the weather was bad, I walked. If there was a typhoon or snow, I was forced to. But I also went on foot when it rained, or even if the forecast simply predicted rain.

Once, I ignored the rain, took my bike, and caught a bad cold. I wouldn't ever make the same mistake again. With that determination, I walked to school whenever rain seemed likely, tucking away my folding umbrella in my school bag.

There was a 60 percent chance of rain that morning, and the sky was heavy with gray clouds. I was walking briskly down a path I usually breezed through on my bike when something caught my eye.

Someone with bright blond hair was standing in a crowd waiting for the light to turn green.

It was Ayase. I could now recognize her, even from behind. She had earphones in, the cables running out from inside her school uniform. She was probably listening to music on the smartphone in her pocket.

She'd done the same thing in PE, and I began to wonder if she had a special interest in it. What did people like her listen to? I was a completely different breed of human, so I couldn't even guess. I didn't imagine we'd have similar tastes, since all I listened to were anime theme songs and Western music.

I briefly considered calling out to her but quickly stopped myself. We'd gone to the trouble of leaving home at different times so we could hide our sibling relationship and keep our lives as they were before our parents married. Talking to each other on the way to or from school, where another student might see us, would run counter to that decision.

The light turned green. No one moved. I didn't, either.

Ayase was the only one who stepped forward.

That was what did it.

"Ayase!"

"Huh?"

The sound of car engines and honking grew louder and louder as if climbing a musical scale, erasing whatever resolve I had to act like a stranger.

There was no time to lose. I couldn't wait a split second. Even that thought occurred *after I'd already moved.*

"...!"

I pulled her arm with all my strength. She staggered backward, unable to maintain her balance. With only average muscle and coordination, I could never support her weight in such an unsteady position.

Ayase and I fell butt-first onto the road in front of the pedestrian crossing.

A large car ran a red light in front of our eyes.

She'd almost died. She'd been seconds away from oblivion, and that was no exaggeration.

"......"

"......"

We stared at each other without a word.

As the moments passed, I began to perspire, and my breath grew ragged.

The people around us watched with concern in their eyes as I got to my feet, took Ayase's hand, and pulled her up.

"Over here," I said. "Come with me for a sec, will you?"

"Huh…? Oh…okay."

Weaving through the crowd and avoiding attention as much as possible, I led her to a back alley where no one would see us.

What I was about to do would embarrass her, and I didn't think it should be done in public. I checked left and right to make sure we were alone, then turned to face her head-on and spoke.

"You can't be doing things like that," I said firmly and quietly.

I wasn't her real brother, and I wasn't in a position to lecture her. That's why I wouldn't warn her even if people thought she was a delinquent or spread rumors about her dating for money.

It didn't matter what they said—that would be going too far. I'd be meddling in her personal affairs, and I wanted to avoid that at all costs. I doubted Ayase wanted me to get that involved in her life, either.

But this was something I couldn't ignore.

"You could have died," I said. "That was really bad. I can't just let you go without a warning."

"…Sorry."

Her voice was troubled and hoarse as I quietly admonished her. Her withdrawn attitude surprised me.

"Oh, uh…sorry," I said. "I didn't mean to sound so bossy."

"N-no, it's my fault."

"Why did you step out into the road? That car was so loud; everyone noticed it and stayed put even when the light turned green."

"Sorry, I wasn't paying attention… I was too focused on what I was listening to."

"Your music? You were doing that in class, too. It's fine to enjoy that kind of thing, but you should be more careful on the road."

I'd wound up lecturing her anyway. Well, whatever. I figured it was okay, since she'd almost died.

"Ah, um, it isn't music… Oh!"

Ayase reached for her ear like she'd just realized something. She didn't find what she was looking for, and she began to glance around.

I noticed it, too.

There was an earphone in one of her ears, but the other had fallen out and was hanging limply from its cable.

It wasn't music that I heard from the device in her pocket. Instead, it was the calm voice of a woman saying something in English.

"You're studying English?" I asked.

"…! S-so what if I am? It's none of your business."

Ayase covered her pocket with a hand and glared at me. For some reason, she was blushing.

"I can't believe it… Are you embarrassed?"

"……"

Her shoulders shook briefly; then she was expressionless again.

We left the back alley and returned to the pedestrian crossing. This time, I carefully checked left and right to ensure no cars were approaching, then began moving across the street. Though Ayase appeared calm, her ears were still red.

"So you want to learn English?" I asked again.

"…Why are you following me?"

"We're going in the same direction."

It was simply inevitable that I would be trailing after her; it didn't mean I had some ulterior motive.

But in reality, I *did* have a reason for following her.

Maybe the pounding in my heart after that near-death experience was making me irrational. Either way, I was having trouble reining in my curiosity about her.

Maybe this was what they called the "suspension bridge effect," where a scary experience amplified one's attraction. Whatever it was, I had to do something about this feeling bubbling up inside my chest.

Ayase didn't seem particularly bothered. Instead, she mumbled, "Well, okay. Whatever," maintained her steady pace, and kept walking.

"It's just part of my studies," she said.

"Huh? What are you talking about?"

"You're the one who asked about the English lessons I was listening to."

She looked at me with a scowl. I had assumed she'd ignored me earlier, but it seemed she was now in the mood to talk.

"For college entrance exams?" I asked.

"That too. But I'm thinking a little further into the future."

"Job hunting, then?"

"We're living in a global age, after all."

Yomiuri would have teased me about being worldly or something if I'd said that. But when Ayase said it, it sounded perfectly natural.

"In that case, there was no reason for you to be embarrassed," I said.

"Of course I was embarrassed. It was like having you see me, a duck, desperately paddling my feet underwater when I'm pretending to be a swan."

"Oh… Are you talking about your armor again?"

"Yeah."

She'd said before that she dyed her hair blond like a bad girl in order to become a powerful, independent woman.

She had probably been listening to the same audio lessons during PE. Skipping class was nothing impressive, but PE grades didn't help you get into college, and Sports Day practice was only good for making fond memories.

If Ayase had decided that was all a waste of time and used the period to study, that seemed right in line with her desire to become a strong, perfect woman.

Ayase was like a puzzle to me, and as I got to know her, I had the sensation I was moving all the mismatched pieces back into their proper spots.

We had left the main street by then, the clumps of tall buildings fading into the background, and we soon caught sight of our high school in the distance.

The silhouettes of passersby had been varied before—men and women, young and old—but now they were more or less uniform. Everyone was around the same age and wore the same school clothes. It was morning rush hour, and we were all headed to class.

Although we didn't see anyone we knew, Ayase's appearance stood out at an elite school like ours, and people were glancing her way.

"Don't tell anyone, okay? …See you later."

With that, Ayase picked up speed.

Maybe she was annoyed at the curious stares of our classmates, or maybe, if she was as kind as I wanted to believe, she was trying to make sure she didn't cause me any trouble.

It didn't matter either way, though. From here on, we would act as promised and pretend to be strangers.

"Okay. Got it," I said to her as she turned her back.

I didn't expect a reply.

But that wasn't a bad thing.

I'd had a lot of excitement that morning, and I was as tired as if it was already the end of the day. Unfortunately, this wasn't a story; it was reality. I couldn't count on some author to conveniently decide I'd done enough for now and skip along to the next morning.

My busy day went on without a break, and with no regard for our emotions, Ayase and I were soon thrust into each other's company once again.

It happened during PE.

It was first period, and we were practicing for Sports Day again, on the same tennis court as before. Only one thing was different.

"Taaaake thaaat!!"

Narasaka's shout was followed by a calm remark from the other side of the court.

"Hey, Maaya, you're hitting the ball too high."

The speaker had been a stranger not long ago, but I now knew her quite well. She was my stepsister.

Ayase, who had been leaning against the fence listening to music—or rather, English lessons, as it turned out—was now engaged in a rally with her friend.

Was it because she had almost died that morning? I didn't know what had caused her change of heart, but she was running around on her side of the court, doing a pretty good job.

"...a...mura."

She had tied her hair back, and it was dancing beautifully in the air like the tail of a thoroughbred horse. Her arms were bare, as were her thighs. Her whole body was firm and tight as she leaped around the court, swinging her racket with precise, economic movement and guiding the ball exactly where she wanted it.

"...ey...atch ou...mura."

I wasn't into tennis or anything, but I could tell that a lot of people's eyes were glued to Ayase's top-class performance. You could barely tell the difference between her and a professional player. I was staring, too, so I was hardly one to judge. But I *did* think ogling a girl in the middle of class instead of focusing on your own game was a good reason for personal reflection. That said, I would happily reflect until the cows came home if that meant I could keep watching. That was how well she played...

"Hey, Asamura!"

"Huh? ...Whoa!"

I heard my best friend yell at me just as a circular shadow shot into my field of vision. I quickly pulled my racket next to my face, just in time for a ball to smack it lightly against my forehead.

It hurt.

"Pay attention, for Pete's sake. That ball isn't as hard as a baseball, but it's dangerous if it hits your head."

Maru came running toward me and picked up the ball as it bounced across the ground. He looked exasperated as he hit his racket against his thick shoulder. The gesture looked inexplicably cool. It really irked me how someone athletic could make simple moves like that look so good.

If you were wondering what Maru, who would be playing softball on

Sports Day, was doing here on the tennis court, that was because we were taking turns using the practice court, and half the time, each group had to play the other group's sport.

This was a problem unique to sports with limited practice space, but it was precisely because of this that guys like Maru, who played on the school team, were allowed to take part. If they weren't, they'd lose out on practice while other students took up the space.

"Sorry," I said. "I was just, uh, you know."

"You were drooling over a girl, weren't you?"

"Has anyone ever told you you're *too* perceptive?"

"Probably. But that's just how I roll, and I don't give a rat's ass about people who can't deal with it."

That was our team's catcher for you. He lived to the beat of his own drum.

He glanced toward the girls, who were happily hitting the ball back and forth.

"Were you watching Ayase? I thought I told you she was bad news…"

"No, you've got it all wrong."

He was right that I was watching Ayase, but it wasn't like he thought. We may only be stepsiblings, but she was still my sister. I didn't have a crush on her or anything. But Maru misinterpreted what I meant.

"Then Maaya? Well, she's all right."

"I'm trying to tell you it isn't like that."

"Don't worry about it, my boy. Maaya's nice. I recommend her. She's bright, lively, and gets along with everyone. She has good grades, and she got an A rating on the practice exam for Waseda University. People say good things about her."

"Don't you know a little too much about her?"

"She's a popular topic. She stands out, though for all the opposite reasons Ayase does. The only downside is that too many guys are after her, and the competition is fierce."

Was it just my imagination, or did Maru seem to talk faster when he spoke about Narasaka? Looking into the placid eyes behind his glasses, I couldn't tell what he was thinking. I wondered briefly if he might have a crush on her but then decided to shelve that thought. I couldn't begin to imagine my best friend becoming infatuated with a girl.

"I don't see Narasaka that way at all," I said. "But if I did, it's doubtful I could beat the competition."

"Ha-ha-ha. Maybe you're right."

"As my friend, you're really supposed to disagree."

"Narasaka's the caring type. See how she's gotten an outcast like Ayase to play tennis with her?"

"I get the feeling she'd go for a solid, serious type of guy."

"Just the opposite. People like her tend to be attracted to losers who need help."

"Then maybe I have a chance."

"...Are you being serious?"

Maru looked at me like I was crazy. I'd only said what came to mind, and I couldn't understand why he was making that face.

"Listen, Asamura. You aren't the loser you think you are."

"Are you trying to say I'm even worse than I think?"

"Whoa, turn down the negativity, okay?"

I flashed him a wry smile—I'd only been joking. He sighed heavily and started scolding me like a wife telling off her husband.

"You're intelligent. At the top of our grade."

"H-hmm. It feels weird when you praise me like that."

"Calm down. Right now, I'm explaining why Narasaka wouldn't like you, so it's more like an insult."

"Either way, could you be a little less straightforward?"

I knew it was Maru's way to be outspoken, but I would have preferred a little more discretion. Not that I cared whether I had a chance to be Narasaka's boyfriend, of course.

".......................................Hmm?"

As we continued to whisper while stealing glances at the girls, I noticed Ayase turn our way. She must have realized we were watching her. Our eyes met for just a moment, and she quickly looked away. That was wise. The other students might have gotten suspicious if we stared at each other for too long. She'd made the right decision.

Still, even a fleeting moment like that was enough for some people to notice.

Maaya Narasaka was one such individual.

I could see why people said she was caring. Some of that probably came from her sharp insight. Ayase and I had met each other's gaze for only a split second, and she must have only seen it out of the corner of her eye, yet she noticed a change in Ayase and shot me a questioning glance. Then she tilted her head a fraction. She looked like a squirrel or a prairie dog—it was cute. I could understand why my classmates liked her.

Come to think of it, I should probably stop staring. Ayase had worked hard to keep people from noticing, and I was putting her effort to waste.

I hastily turned away.

"Weren't you saying you didn't see her that way?" Maru asked.

"I don't. Really."

"Hmm. Guess you're a guy after all."

"Remarks like that are problematic and likely to give people the wrong idea."

"So it's just typical high-school-boy lust, then."

"I don't think I like your choice of words!"

"Of course, I don't think you're the kind of guy who would carelessly act on his carnal passions. But don't worry—your heart belongs to you alone. You're free to think whatever you want."

Maru had to be teasing me. I was sure of it.

"Okay, all right. I appreciate your understanding," I said with a sigh and a shrug.

The two girls, meanwhile, appeared to have noticed me watching them, and it seemed too late to try to act casual about it.

"Finished?" Maru asked me.

"Oh yeah. I'm going to go practice."

For the remainder of the period, I managed to regain my focus and spent the time practicing hard.

The girls' class ended earlier, since it took them longer to get changed, and by the time I looked at the next tennis court over, it was empty, with only a single yellow ball on the ground.

The bell rang as silver beads of rain started pouring down, the gray sky unable to hold back the shower any longer. The fallen droplets created a mottled pattern on the court.

"I didn't think it would rain," Maru said as he jogged over to me. "Come on, let's get back inside."

"Really?" I said. "The weather forecast said there was a sixty percent chance."

I didn't want to get wet, either, and we ran side by side back to the school building.

"I'm more than happy to bet on forty percent," Maru said. "How many baseball players do you think there are in the world who bat four hundred?!"

"I'm not sure that has anything to do with the weather."

Was he saying 40 percent was good enough from a baseball player's perspective? Maybe the same numbers simply held different value for different people. No, there was definitely something wrong with Maru's thought process.

"Hurry, Asamura! The rain's getting worse!"

We ran inside just as it began to pour. Maru turned around and glared at the sky.

"It isn't going to stop. I guess we'll have to work with weights inside today..."

He bent his huge body forward and sneezed.

The schoolyard had already turned a dark brown. The heavy rain blurred the scenery like fog. The pounding of the drops seemed like the only sound in the world.

"It's already June," I remarked. "Time for the rainy season."

"Still, batting four hundred is batting four hundred," Maru shot back. "You would expect a hit."

"That's ridiculous."

The clouds overhead were a dark gray, and just as Maru said, it didn't look like it would stop anytime soon. I was glad I'd brought my umbrella. I should be able to reach home without getting wet.

...Or so I thought at the time.

School was out, and of course, it was still raining.

I'd been right, not that I was happy about it. Predictions you don't want to come true usually do. Murphy's Law was alive and well.

Fortunately, I was off work that day and didn't have to head out to Shibuya Station. I figured it'd be wise to go straight home. Just as I was moving toward the shoe lockers by the front entrance, I spotted a familiar figure.

A girl was looking up at the rainy sky. The backdrop of gray clouds dulled the bright color of her hair.

*That's Ayase...isn't it? Don't tell me she forgot her umbrella.* The forecast had said there was a 60 percent chance of rain. I wanted to ask her if she was another baseball fan who appreciated a .400 batting average, but then I remembered something. She had left home before I did. She was already out the door when I checked the weather report.

Watching her profile from a distance, I wondered what to do.

I looked left and right. The coast was clear. Everyone appeared to have gone home early—a wise choice.

I opened my bag and pulled out the folding umbrella at the bottom. A folding umbrella fits easily in a school bag, so it's not a hassle to carry it. The only question was whether to bring it. Who was it who said life was a series of choices?

I walked noisily over to Ayase so I wouldn't scare her and stopped about three steps away. This was about the right distance. I didn't have the nerve to tap her shoulder from behind. I mean, I was a guy, and it wouldn't be right to touch a girl's body like that. Besides, my peaceful school days would be ruined if she screamed.

I cleared my throat before speaking.

"Do you want to share my umbrella?"

Her shoulders shook, and she turned around, making her golden-colored hair dance. It reflected the faint fluorescent light from the ceiling, and the silver earring in her ear flashed.

She turned her blank stare on me, slowly focusing on my face. Then, like a computer system that had safely restarted, emotion returned to her expression.

"Huh?"

Her eyes widened in surprise. *Is this so shocking?* I wondered.

"Have you forgotten who I am?" I asked.

"What are you talking about, Asamura?"

"That's what I'd like to ask you."

I was getting a little nervous.

"So what do you want?" she asked. "We're still at school, and you're talking to me."

"Oh, um, well."

She wasn't upset. I understood that much. It was more like she was suspicious. Over the last few days, I'd learned a little about how to read her expressions. I knew we'd decided to act like strangers at school. But it didn't make sense to criticize me for breaking that rule. We were really siblings, so there was no reason to feel guilty.

Ayase had the intelligence and logic to reach that rational conclusion, and so she'd asked me what I wanted. That was a big help. If she sounded a little short, it was probably the awkwardness from that morning. Or at least I hoped it was.

"Did you forget your umbrella?" I asked, returning to the subject at hand.

"Oh... Yeah, kinda."

"Batting four hundred, huh?"

"What's that supposed to mean?"

Confused, she glanced at the umbrella in my hand.

"We're going to the same place," I said, "so I figured we might as well share."

I was trying to say there was no reason for her to hold back if it meant getting wet. My message should have been clear.

She looked taken aback, or perhaps troubled.

"Oh... No. I'm meeting a friend. She said she had to stop by her clubroom. So it's okay..."

"In that case..." I spoke rapidly and kept to the point. "You can use this. I won't get too wet if I run home."

Before she could argue, I pushed the umbrella into her hand, put on my shoes, and ran out into the rain.

Now I'd done it, I thought. Maybe I was meddling in her affairs.

She'd said she was waiting for a friend. Maybe she was planning to share an umbrella with her. But would they manage to stay dry doubling up? Girls' umbrellas tended to be small.

I kept remembering the blank look on Ayase's face when I'd forced her to take my umbrella. It was as if she'd never dreamed that I'd do something like that. Just seeing the look on her face had made it worthwhile to me.

It was yet another expression of hers that I hadn't seen before.

I wondered if we'd keep revising our behavior and compromising until we became real siblings. That was the thought occupying my mind as I ran home.

The pelting June rain soaked through my school uniform. A cold liquid that I knew wasn't sweat slid down my back. The rain pooled in my shoes, causing an uncomfortable squishing sensation with every step I took.

I was relieved to finally see our tall apartment building emerge from behind the silver curtain of rain.

I opened the self-locking door, walked past the super's office, and took the corner elevator to the third floor. A wet splish-splash sound echoed in the hallway as I made my way past several doors and reached home at last.

I unlocked the door, went inside, and turned on the light.

An orange glow filled the space, and I mumbled, "I'm home..."

There was no response—only silence. But that was only natural, since Dad and Akiko weren't home yet. I should have gotten used to it a long time ago.

For some reason, though, I'd begun to feel a little lonely when I didn't get a reply.

I tossed my school bag on the dining table and headed straight to the bathroom.

Twisting the faucet, I began drawing a bath. I'd let it fill for about fifteen minutes.

During that time, I hung my uniform on a hanger and threw my wet clothes into the washing machine. I measured the required detergent and fabric softener and turned it on. Water poured into the drum, and it began noisily rotating.

"Oops, I almost forgot."

I needed to put out some underwear. Otherwise, I'd be walking around with nothing but a towel on after bathing. That may have been acceptable before, but not anymore.

Was that kind of thing okay if you were real siblings? No. No way.

Right?

I slipped into the tub when it was about half-filled, waiting blankly for the hot water to climb up the surface of my skin. I turned off the faucet when it was up to my shoulders.

The hot water stung a little. The June rain seemed to have chilled my entire body. I sighed—I sounded exhausted. The heat of the bath made my thoughts fuzzy as I remembered Ayase's request.

She wanted a part-time job that paid well. Since she'd agreed to cook for me, I had to find her something to keep up my end of our deal.

I recalled how she'd said she liked to give a lot when it came to give-and-take. Now that I knew that, I couldn't let her pamper me. I felt the same way she did. So I had to find her a job.

"Hmm..."

As I thought about it, I slapped the water's surface with the palm of my hand for no particular reason. In today's world, maybe it was better to start a business than to be an employee. It had said on the cover of one of the books I'd picked out that you made better money hiring than you did being hired.

In that case, maybe becoming a YouTuber or delivering food for Uber...? ...No, that wasn't the answer. I needed to calm down and think.

As a student, I didn't know the first thing about starting a business. There was too much I needed to learn. Maru was right. You had to understand the mechanisms of society and how to do business...which I knew nothing about. Finding a high-paying part-time job was starting to seem impossible.

But in that case, I couldn't ask Ayase to continue cooking my meals. It wouldn't be fair. We'd have to start taking turns.

That said, I didn't have her skills. I conjured up a hazy image of her wearing an apron over her school uniform. She looked cute— No, not cute. It didn't turn me on; it just...suited her. Yeah, that was it.

She pulled up her long hair and tied it at the nape of her neck, her gaze straight ahead. Then she tugged once on the loose end of the hair tie where it lay on her shoulder. And the next thing you knew, she was chopping away on the cutting board.

Her practiced motions were proof that this was something she had done repeatedly. She must have. She had probably been cooking for years, while I bought ready-made meals at convenience stores or ordered delivery. And I was pretty sure it hadn't been for her own benefit.

My dad had no idea how to cook, so he didn't mind that I was the same. But Akiko wasn't like that. It was easy to see from the food she had prepared on our first day together that she had tried to feed her daughter as many homemade meals as possible. That wasn't to say one way was better than the other; that was just the kind of person she was. I wouldn't have minded at all if Akiko didn't cook.

But as a result, if Ayase had always ordered food when Akiko wasn't home, I presume her mother would have done anything to cook for her.

To ensure her busy mom wouldn't feel compelled to do that, Ayase had to be able to cook when she wasn't there. That must have been why she'd learned. That's what I thought, anyway, and I was probably right. It was simply a matter of observation and thought. If you kept doing that, you could figure out a lot about someone. But of course, you had to have a reason to think about such things.

"Armor…huh."

Ayase had been fighting while I had been running away.

"I'd really like to find her that high-paying gig…"

My mind had gone back to the subject of jobs, but no brilliant ideas came to mind. I was thinking so hard that my head was heating up. I felt dizzy.

I left the tub, shampooed the stickiness from the rain out of my hair, washed my body, and exited the bathroom. I checked the washing machine and saw that the spin cycle was done, and it was now in dry mode. It was a little noisy, but there was nothing I could do about that. Besides, it wasn't so late that I needed to start worrying about annoying the neighbors.

I put on some light cotton indoor clothes and decided to stop worrying for the time being. The cool air flowing into the hall from the living room air conditioner felt good against my hot skin. It brightened my mood, and I started humming as I headed toward it. It was then that I finally realized I hadn't turned on the air conditioner.

Two girls were standing in the living room, and they turned to look at me. It was Ayase and…Narasaka?

Why were they here?

My mind went blank momentarily; then I realized… Dang it! I'd forgotten I was living with a stepsister and started humming to myself…!

Embarrassment hit me like an invading army, and I couldn't even put up a fight. My face grew hot. I could tell I was flushing from ear to ear.

Narasaka was there, too—a total stranger. She had definitely seen—or rather, heard me. Ugh. I could die a hundred times from embarrassment alone. *What the heck should I do?* I was numb down to my toes, and I couldn't move.

Narasaka's mouth hung open. Her lips were frozen in an "oh" shape.

"Sorry," Ayase said, inching toward me and whispering, "Maaya wanted to see my new home. I meant to warn you, but I don't have your contact info."

So she wasn't able to reach me.

She folded her hands together in apology, which was unusual. Perhaps she felt more relaxed with her friend around.

After looking stunned for a moment, Narasaka went back to smiling like always.

"Whoa!" she exclaimed. "You must be the big brother Saki's been telling me about! So it *is* you—Yuuta Asamura from the next class over!"

She was full of energy.

"Hey, do you know who I am?" she continued. "Has Saki told you about me?"

"Uh...yeah." What was I supposed to say? "She told me you two were friendly."

I figured a neutral response was a safe bet, though I thought I saw a brief change in Narasaka's eyes when she heard me.

"Oh, 'friendly,' huh?" she said in a quiet voice. I may have been mistaken, since I was only reading her lips, but her face looked almost serious...maybe a little troubled. Ayase probably didn't notice, since she had come over to me and had her back to Narasaka.

But the other girl's clouded expression was gone in an instant. It might sound stupid to phrase it like this, but her face brightened like a flower in full bloom.

"Yeah! We're good buddies!" she said. "So I hope we can get along, too, Asamura!"

"Uh...sure. Same to you. Were the two of you okay in the rain, by the way?"

It was still pouring outside. I wouldn't call it a storm, but the wind was blowing, and the raindrops were falling at an angle against the window.

"We were fine!" Narasaka said. "We both had umbrellas!"

"I see."

"Saki said she'd forgotten hers, but she found it."

"It was at the bottom of my bag," said Ayase.

So that's how she'd explained it. I was glad it wasn't too obviously a man's umbrella.

"Ooh, you scatterbrain!" Narasaka exclaimed.

"I start experiencing psychogenic vertigo when you say things like that," Ayase shot back.

"You're using big words again! Does anyone even talk like that these days?"

"Huh? Is it weird?"

"Yeah! But it's okay."

Narasaka leaped onto the couch, sending her skirt fluttering. Ayase sighed at her bad manners.

"Maaya. Your underwear is showing."

"Oh!"

Panicking, Narasaka jumped up and straightened her skirt, then glared at me suspiciously. *No, Narasaka, I didn't see anything. The angle wasn't right.*

"Saki, this place is dangerous," she said.

"What're you talking about?" Ayase asked.

"There's a guy here!"

"I suppose Asamura doesn't look much like a girl."

"He's a guy. A male!"

"So what?"

"What're you going to do?! You can't walk around in your underwear after taking a bath!"

"I don't walk around in my underwear. Is that what you do?"

"Of course not. I'm a lady."

For some reason, Narasaka sounded really proud as she said this.

"But hey, Saki?"

"Wh-what?"

"It's nice to hear you talk to me so casually."

"...!"

Ayase quickly turned away, but it was too late for that now. She'd been caught totally off guard. I could tell she was blushing.

"Wow, that's so sweet of you," said Narasaka. "Your father is so pleased."

"Maaya, you aren't my father!"

It sounded like Ayase usually used polite language with Maaya, but she'd slipped up just now.

"It took so long for you to call me by my first name, too."

"Yeah?"

"Yeah!"

"I've already forgotten."

"Well, I remember!"

"You can erase it from your memory."

"No way!"

Narasaka looked pleased, but I didn't think it was because Ayase was being casual with her. It seemed to me like she was happy that Ayase was revealing her true self.

Some people liked to show off how tight they were with their friends by being rude to them, taking casual closeness too far. But rudeness was rudeness, whether you were friends or not.

Ayase and I had agreed to keep calling each other by our surnames, as we did at school. That was because we didn't have any negative feelings about continuing to address each other politely, despite the fact that we had agreed to dispense with formal language.

Narasaka seemed like someone who would understand that.

No, maybe I was wrong. How could I know that about her? This was the first time we'd spoken to each other. But at the same time, if she was the type to misunderstand our situation, I didn't think Ayase would have made friends with her or invited her to our house. That's how I saw it anyway. As I said before, you can understand a lot through observation and thought.

"Anyway!" said Narasaka. "Nice to meet you, Big Brother!"

"B-Brother?"

Hadn't she called me *Asamura* a moment ago? Her sudden chummy attitude was making me reconsider what I'd just thought about her.

"Don't be shy, Big Brother!"

"Uh, I'm not your brother…"

"Oh, come on, we're practically family now. You can call me Maaya, too."

"I'm not sure I'm ready for that. And family? I'm Ayase's stepbrother, not yours."

"Don't sweat the small stuff, Big Brother! It's nice being called that, isn't it?"

"Not really."

Some people might feel that way, but not me. Though, hearing "Big Brother" repeated in Narasaka's sweet voice was a little like having a tiny animal take a liking to me.

At any rate, Narasaka was bolder than I'd thought. She hadn't seemed the type to start pestering her friend's brother.

"…Stop it…," a faint voice said. Ayase had her head down like she was under attack. "…It's embarrassing."

"Speak up!" said Narasaka. "I can't hear you!"

"I said, stop it! It's embarrassing! I get shivers down my spine whenever you say, 'Big Brother.' Please stop calling him that!"

"Oh, wow. You didn't even last as long as he did."

Oh, so that was it.

"You were just teasing me to get a rise out of Ayase, weren't you?" I asked.

"Ah-ha-ha-ha-ha-ha! Bingo!" Narasaka replied.

"Don't *bingo* me," I said.

I wished she wouldn't point at me with that serious look on her face. Or rather, she shouldn't point at people in the first place. It was rude.

"Okay, I'll hold off on making fun of you for now, *Big Brother.*"

"Hold off on it forever. Please."

"Aw, that's no fun. Come on, Saki, try calling him *Big Brother.* On the count of three—"

"Never!" she cried.

"But getting a stepbrother is such a fun life event. You should use it wisely."

"Stop making it sound like I drew a card from the Game of Life... Now what are you doing?"

Narasaka was opening the gym bag she'd slid under the table and pulling something out.

"Here we go. Let's play a game!"

"You brought a game console?" said Ayase.

"Narasaka," I scolded. "You aren't supposed to take games to school..."

"It's not against the rules to bring them," she replied. "We just can't play them."

I didn't see a difference between taking games to school and playing them, but according to Narasaka, it was fine as long as you didn't get it out during class. She said she'd even checked with a teacher, which impressed me. It appeared that Suisei High gave students more freedom than I'd thought.

The console she'd pulled out was the newest model everyone was talking about.

"Saki, you said you didn't have this."

"I don't."

"That's why I wanted to play with you," Narasaka said, pointing to the fifty-inch LCD screen facing the couch. "Can I connect it to your TV?"

"...I don't see why not."

"It has games we can play together. Oh, do you guys have Wi-Fi?"

Ayase eyed me. She was asking if she could give Narasaka the password.

I had given it to her when she first moved in. Nowadays, this was like a ritual that everyone performed when they handed someone a key to their house. I nodded.

Ayase wrote down the password and gave it to Narasaka, who quickly set up the game system and returned to the couch.

"Do you want to play with us?" she asked, turning to me.

She pulled more objects out of her bag. There were two—no, three controllers. Was one of them for me? I recalled what Maru had said about

Narasaka being considerate. Maybe she'd been planning to have me join in from the outset.

I made eye contact with Ayase again, asking her what to do.

"Well, it still hasn't stopped raining," she said, "so we might as well. Feel free to jump in, Asamura."

Ayase slid over to the end of the couch and made room for me.

"Oh-ho. So Saki wants to sit next to her *big brother*, I see."

"Never mind," said Ayase, sliding back to where she'd been sitting before. "Make room for him on your side, will you?"

"He can sit between us," said Narasaka. "How's that, Asamura? You'll have a beauty on each arm!"

"I'd prefer to sit at the end…"

"Uh-uh," said Narasaka. "It's nonnegotiable."

"Seems a little weird for you to be grabbing on to our couch like you own it," Ayase muttered, looking exasperatedly at her friend, who was gripping the opposite armrest with all her might.

"Okay, okay. I'll sit wherever you want me to sit," I said.

Without much choice, I plopped down in the middle.

It wasn't a big couch. Three people could barely squeeze in. We hadn't needed anything bigger, since it had always been just my dad and me.

At any rate, you could hardly expect me to stay calm, seated between two girls who were both the subject of gossip throughout my school. I might do my best to put on a neutral face, but there was a limit to my endurance.

"Mm, Asamura, you smell lovely fresh out of the bath," commented Narasaka. "I guess it's your shampoo. Saki must use the same kind."

"Of course I don't," said Ayase. "Use your common sense."

I didn't know it was common sense to use a different shampoo from your brother. Come to think of it, it had never even occurred to me to use a different shampoo or bodywash from Dad. I'd have to be more careful when I went shopping. Ayase seemed to have read my mind, however.

"I can buy stuff for myself. I'm not a little kid."

The way she paid attention and was quick to reassure me really made my life easier.

"Okay, let's get to it!"

Narasaka began maneuvering her controller.

I heard lively music start up and focused my attention on the screen.

I'd sat on this couch countless times before, so why did it seem like I was the most uncomfortable right now? I recalled what Ayase had said earlier—she'd referred to it as *our couch*. She probably hadn't meant anything by it, but her words had made me happy.

We launched the game. It took a second to search for the latest patches online but soon got underway without any updates.

"Hey, is this...a scary game, by any chance?"

Ayase's voice took on a hint of tension.

"It isn't scary," said Narasaka. "It's a cute game, like a puzzle! You control this squishy character, make it hold hands with other characters, and aim for the finish line over here." She pointed to a human-shaped character that was wobbling like it didn't have a bone in its body.

With a move of her controller, Narasaka made her character fly into the air, pivot, and land in a patch of thorns. Blood splattered everywhere, and the character screamed and fell beneath the stage.

"See? Your character dies when something like that happens."

"It *is* a horror game!" Ayase exclaimed.

"No, it isn't! You can reach the finish line if you do it right. It's only scary if you make a mistake. Here, Asamura, use this one," Narasaka said, handing me a controller. "Listen up, everyone: The important thing is that we stay in sync. It'll be like cutting the cake together at a wedding!"

"Isn't that something brides and grooms do?" Ayase said sarcastically.

"Oh, stop complaining! Here we go!"

Heaps of characters died.

That was to be expected; it was my first time, so I wasn't going to be great at it. But every time I lost a character, Narasaka would get excited and say, "*Hey, you're almost there! Come on, don't panic. Keep going! Oh, shoot!*" And every time, she bumped her shoulder against mine.

We were awfully close to each other. She acted way more like my kid sister than Ayase did.

"Phew! Great game!" said Narasaka when it was over.

It had stopped raining by the time we were finished playing. Our guest went home looking utterly content.

"I'm sorry my friend's so annoying," Ayase said once she'd seen Narasaka out the door.

"Oh, no worries."

"Hey..."

Ayase seemed to have trouble getting out what she wanted to say, so I asked her what was on her mind.

"Can we exchange contact info?" she said at last. "That way, we can avoid any trouble in the future, you know?"

"Oh yeah. Okay."

I had nothing against the idea. It was necessary to avoid unfortunate situations going forward. Besides, we were family. Exchanging contact info was by no means unusual.

I opened my phone and saw Ayase's icon in my friends list.

She was using a photo of a fancy teacup. It was only an icon, but it seemed typical of her to choose something that didn't give away her gender.

"I wonder if this is also a kind of armor..."

"Did you say something?" Ayase said, turning toward me from the kitchen.

She'd gone straight there after we exchanged info. I heard her knife stop on the cutting board for a second when she spoke.

"Oh, nothing."

"Dinner will be ready soon," she said.

"Okay."

Ayase resumed cutting, and the aroma of miso soup tickled my nostrils.

I thought back to the busy day I'd had. It'd been one thing after another, starting on my way to school when I'd discovered what Ayase had been listening to on her earphones.

Later, I'd watched Ayase having a friendly tennis match with Narasaka. Then I'd gotten soaked despite taking my umbrella to school. I made the biggest mistake of my life humming after my bath in front of a stranger, and then I'd been unable to show off when playing games with Narasaka and Ayase.

Still, I felt like it'd been a good day, and I'd gained a lot.

With that thought, I turned off my phone's screen.

# ● JUNE 11 (THURSDAY)

It was morning, and the four members of our family, including Akiko, were seated around the dining table.

She had come home late last night—or should I say, this morning—and should have still been in bed.

"The summer solstice is coming up," she said, letting out an airy little yawn.

She said the bright sunlight coming in through the window had woken her up. *Maybe we should get blackout curtains for the main bedroom.* I decided to bring it up with Dad. I bet he hadn't even thought about it.

Akiko stepped into the kitchen, saying she'd go back to bed later. As for Dad, he was starting late that day, so he was taking more time than usual reading the latest business news on his tablet.

And so, all four of us were eating together for once.

"Here, Dad. You wipe that side."

"Okay."

I tossed a cleaning cloth to him. Smiling, he carefully wiped the surface of his and Akiko's half of the table.

Once it was clean, Akiko and Ayase brought over breakfast. There was a greater variety of foods, since Akiko had helped out.

The last dish was Japanese omelets. These required a square frying pan, which we didn't have before. Akiko had brought one when she moved in. To make them, you spread a thin layer of egg mixture on a heated pan and rolled it up neatly using cooking chopsticks. I had watched as Akiko made them, but I didn't think I could ever manage a feat like that. Ayase had stood next to her, tasting the miso soup on the stove and staring at her mom's handiwork like an apprentice, eager to steal her master's techniques.

Expressing our thanks for the meal, we all sat down at the table and reached for the food with our chopsticks.

Without thinking, I moved my hand toward the beautifully browned omelets that Akiko had made. I picked up a thick slice—the cross section was the same yellow as Naruto's hair. The juice spread in my mouth with the first bite. It wasn't what I had expected.

"This is great! But...is it not an omelet?"

"It's *dashimaki tamago*."

Akiko had made it, but Ayase was the one who answered.

"*Dashimaki tamago*?" I repeated.

"Normally, omelets only taste like eggs, right?" she continued. "You can add salt if you like it savory or sugar if you prefer it sweet."

"Sugar?"

"You don't like it sweet? Then I'll make sure not to add sugar when I make them."

"Oh, I mean...either way is fine. I just didn't know people ate sweet omelets."

"Huh...?" said Ayase, seeming surprised.

"What?" Akiko, too, seemed taken aback.

They didn't have to look at me like some being from another world.

"...You've taken home economics, right?" asked Ayase.

"Oh, um, yeah," I said. "But we didn't make omelets. We made fried eggs instead."

"Hmm. You make *dashimaki tamago* by cooking eggs in dashi—that's a broth."

"Dashi...? Is that like the soup base you use for noodles?"

"Well, we use white dashi, which is a little different."

I glanced toward the kitchen and noticed an unfamiliar white bottle on the counter. That was probably what she was talking about. Akiko must have brought that, too, since my dad and I never cooked and only had salt, soy sauce, and sugar.

"You're tasting the broth added to the eggs," said Ayase. "We could also use salt or a little mirin to make it sweet. You can throw in some soy sauce, too, but that would darken the color, and the omelets wouldn't come out a pretty yellow like these."

"You sure know a lot about this stuff."

"Saki can make it, too," Akiko chimed in. "Saki, why don't you make it for Yuuta if he likes it?"

"I can't make them this fluffy…"

"I'm fine with fried eggs, too," I said.

"…Okay. Well, I'll make it for you if the mood strikes me."

I'll explain what Ayase and I were really saying with that exchange: First, I told her she didn't have to add to the work she was already doing under our agreement and that I was fine with how things were. In response, Ayase thanked me and said she'd make *dashimaki tamago* to show her appreciation if she had the time.

It was convenient that we could communicate between the lines like that, though I'd double-check later just in case, since misunderstandings could occur easily when you spoke in code.

Meanwhile, Dad was oblivious to our exchange, rambling on and on about how delicious Akiko's *dashimaki tamago* was. Personally, I think he was going a little too far when he said it was the best in the world. Was he bragging about how skilled his new wife was? Was this how people acted when they were in love? I never dreamed that I'd hear my dad, over forty, bragging about his wife first thing in the morning. This dealt some serious psychic damage to a sixteen-year-old like me.

I started thinking hard, trying to come up with any other topic, and remembered something.

"Hey, I think it's my turn to do the laundry this week. I can add in Akiko's and Ayase's, too, right?"

"Oh, uh, wait…"

Ayase stammered and swallowed the rest of what she had started to say.

I tilted my head curiously. It was rare for someone as straightforward as Ayase to act this way. What was going on? Had I said something weird?

"Um, Yuuta," Akiko began. "I'll do all the laundry if that's fine with you."

"Huh? But I don't want to trouble you."

The four of us had discussed sharing the household chores when we decided to live together. A lot had changed since then, but I didn't want to add to Akiko's workload...

But Akiko persisted. "Doing laundry for four people is a lot of work, you know?"

I was beginning to realize that something was off.

Come to think of it, it was probably insensitive for me, a guy, to wash the women's clothes. My desire to be fair about sharing household duties had been so strong that I had totally overlooked such subtleties.

That was my big mistake. It'd taken so long for me to figure out what Akiko was getting at, Ayase felt she had to speak up and offer a more detailed explanation.

"I don't know about having you wash our underwear...and, um, the fabric is pretty delicate, so it would be tough for you to handle. For example, Asamura, do you know which items go in which laundry nets?"

"...Which *what*?" I asked in genuine confusion. I probably should have just apologized instead for making her say all that.

"The band and straps on a bra will get stretched out if you don't wash them in a bag, and the hooks can damage other fabrics. That's why we have washing bags for them. The same goes for pan—...underpants, where the decorations can come off..."

Despite the awkwardness, she carefully explained the details. I successfully got the message that washing women's clothes was more complicated than I'd thought.

"It's not that different from menswear," she continued. "I'm sure you separate white clothes from dark ones and use a washing bag for puff-print shirts, right? The prints would peel off if you didn't."

"Puff print? You mean like T-shirts with pictures and logos that look kind of 3D?" I asked.

"Exactly."

"Oh, so that's why they peel off whenever I wash them."

Ayase held her head in her hands. After a moment, she looked back up.

"I can't allow you to wash my clothes if you don't even know that," she declared flatly. "I'll just do it myself."

"Oh, okay... Got it."

Akiko smiled sweetly as if to clear the awkwardness.

"I'll do Taichi's clothes when it's my turn to do the laundry," she said. "I can wash your clothes, too, if you like, Yuuta."

I'd been thinking of doing the laundry as simply emptying the laundry basket into the machine, but now a whole complicated process flashed vividly in front of my eyes.

Akiko...

...would wash my underwear?

Whoa. No way. I couldn't let her.

"...Ayase, I think I understand how you feel," I said.

"See?" She sighed.

*It's so obvious now.* I mentally apologized to her.

When I opened the front door, the sound of pounding water coming from across the outside hallway suddenly became much louder. It was raining again today.

Ayase had said she would go to school with me, and we walked out the door together.

I wondered what she wanted. She had been adamant about leaving before me up until now.

We might only be stepsiblings, but she was my sister, so there should be no issue. But wait, was that really true? A boy and his sister still walking together in high school seemed pretty unusual. Or was I just overthinking things?

"I want to talk to you about something," she said as our elevator descended.

Okay, that made sense. It was different if she had a specific reason, and it was just like her to be so straightforward.

"I want to apologize."

"...Apologize?"

What for? I thought about our discussion that morning. Had she done anything that warranted an apology? Of course, there was no mistaking that *I'd* caused offense, but what had she done...?

We stepped out of the elevator and left our apartment building.

The rain seemed to form a cage around us, and few people were out; ours were the only umbrellas as we headed for school. It was the perfect opportunity to talk alone.

The trees that lined the road appeared a rich shade of green in the rain. Cars occasionally passed, honking their horns beyond them. Each time, we stopped and waited, wary of being splashed with puddles.

Once we resumed walking, Ayase frowned and started speaking.

"I have a tendency to make discriminatory remarks without realizing it," she said, her face stern. "It's what I hate most about myself. So I'm sorry."

I tensed up a little, understanding from her expression that this was a serious conversation.

She took in a deep breath and then said all at once, "It isn't impossible that you might wear designer lingerie."

I was pretty sure that *was* impossible.

"All my life, I've scoffed at stereotypical gender roles," she continued.

"Ayase, wait a sec."

"You're pretty careful about grooming. Yesterday, you washed your wet clothes as soon as you got home. I have yet to see you wear lipstick or foundation, but you might like being stylish in ways that aren't obvious."

"Ayase, wait. Calm down."

I walked around her and blocked her path.

The quickest way to keep someone's mind from running wild was to prevent any related action. Made to stop in her tracks, Ayase gasped and raised her head from under her umbrella.

"…Okay. I've calmed down," she said.

"All right, then."

"I know—just because someone likes the idea of cross-dressing, it doesn't mean they actually do it."

It hadn't worked; she was still going.

"Let's take it slow," I said. "You know what our bathroom sink looks like and what's there, right?"

She furrowed her brow and thought this over.

"Um…yeah. There's a shaver and shaving lotion. As for women's cosmetics…none."

"See?"

"But you have shapely brows."

"Huh?"

"They look so nice; you must brush and trim them. I haven't seen an eyebrow comb around, but you could be going to a beauty salon, and—"

"I go to a barbershop."

Going to a beauty salon seemed pretty intimidating for a high school guy. Just because we were in Shibuya, the center of youth culture, didn't mean everyone was into cosmetics and brand-name items. I'd rather buy books if I had that kind of money to spend.

"What? Then you don't touch up your eyebrows?" she asked.

"No, I don't."

She took a good look at them.

"I can't believe it. I'm jealous…"

"Y-you are?"

"…It's not fair."

With that, Ayase began walking again. I followed her without a word. Then after a while, I called out to her.

"Hey."

"What?"

"About what you were saying about gender roles."

"Yeah?"

"You mean like playing the part you're expected to according to your gender, right?"

Putting it roughly, gender roles were the way men and women were supposed to act according to their gender. Unfortunately, the "correct" way to do things was determined by a shared fantasy called society, not by individuals, and often with no concrete reasoning.

"Yeah," she said. "But these days, gender isn't really confined to two categories anymore, right?"

"Oh, well, yeah."

This idea wasn't completely foreign to me. If you read, you'd end up learning about stuff like that, and besides, the topic was often in the news recently. I recalled a report saying the American version of Facebook offered fifty-eight custom gender options. When you really thought about it, DNA wasn't simply male or female, either. It appeared that Ayase was thinking along similar lines.

"Sex chromosomes determine a person's biological sex...," she began.

"Yeah. X chromosomes and Y chromosomes."

"Exactly. Humans have X and Y chromosomes, and their combinations determine a person's sex. Females have two X chromosomes, and males have one X and one Y chromosome. It comes down to just one of the forty-six chromosomes that makes us human, and the only difference is a single X or Y. I wonder what percentage of the genome that is."

She sounded frustrated. This attitude struck me as very like her.

"Well, one thing is for sure," I said. "The difference is very small."

"But that tiny difference is made into such a big deal, and when you think about it, those two categories aren't even absolute."

It was raining hard, but I could hear Ayase's voice loud and clear.

"That goes for gender identity, too," she said. "There are always people whose genders don't match what their DNA says and all sorts of ways to recognize it."

I understood in my head what Ayase was talking about. But I'd been male since I was born, and my DNA agreed, as did my brain. So it all seemed a little abstract.

"It's the same with relationships. A person might like men, women, or both, or not like either. Or they might not want to get into a relationship in the first place... Those are all valid possibilities, and none should be denied. That's true of the way people dress, too. A person can be biologically female, identify as a woman, have a relationship with a man, and still prefer to wear men's clothing. There's nothing unusual about that. Likewise, there's nothing wrong with a man choosing to wear women's underwear."

"Well, sure."

"Yet back then, in the moment, none of that even crossed my mind," she said, frowning. She was clearly disappointed with herself.

I understood the problem. It was one of those things where you were correct from a macro perspective, but if you examined the issue in more detail, you could find infinite exceptions. There was a big difference between making a general statement about most people and saying a single person must be a specific way because that was the norm.

If I *was* the type of guy who wore women's underwear every day and I had a sister with no knowledge of lingerie, wouldn't I be in the same position as Ayase?

She probably didn't mind having her mom wash her clothes. Yet earlier that morning, she'd imagined me washing her underwear and gotten so reflexively embarrassed that she didn't even stop to confirm the details first.

Most people would take that for granted, but Ayase was beating herself up over it.

She was always fighting.

She didn't approve of blindly accepting the roles society pushed on her. She wanted to think everything through. To a guy like me, who just accepted things as they came, she was *dazzling*.

"Well, since you've brought it up," I said, "I was also embarrassed when I imagined Akiko washing my stuff."

"It doesn't matter what anyone else does. I simply can't forgive myself, and I wanted to apologize."

"Hmm."

I briefly pondered that.

I agreed with her ideas, but her seriousness was bound to make things tough for her. I wondered if there was another way of thinking that would make life a little easier without denying the way she felt.

We were coming up on the school gate. Other students would be around, so we couldn't keep talking like this.

"...There's such a thing as reflexes, you know," I said.

"Huh? Like your reflection in a mirror?"

"Reflexes. Not *reflection*."

I sometimes had trouble keeping up with Ayase's train of thought, though I didn't really mind, since it was interesting.

"I mean actions that occur without thought."

"Oh, that. Like your legs moving when someone hits your knee?"

"Yeah, like that."

Some human reactions happen before you have time to think. For example, you close your eyes when something comes flying at you or pull your hand back when you touch something hot.

"I've thought before about why humans still rely on reflexes when we evolved by developing conscious thought," I said.

"Oh...isn't it because we wouldn't have time to avoid danger if we stopped to think?"

"Right. We're made to act before we think when chances are high that our life may be at risk. I think that ability is necessary for all living creatures."

"But what does that have to do with...? Oh, I get it."

Ayase was smart and appeared to have figured things out before I finished explaining. Nonetheless, I continued:

"It's like the macros or shortcut keys in an app."

Ayase chuckled.

"That's an interesting way to put it," she said.

"We use them because they're quick and convenient. But there are cases when a macro doesn't help. At times like that, you won't know what to do, or how to create a different macro, unless you know the basic reasoning behind them."

"Okay."

"I think sometimes, you can't help reacting on reflex. After all, that reaction can benefit you."

"Still, bias breeds discrimination."

"That's why we reexamine things. You thought over the actions you took, then reflected. I don't think you should have to keep worrying beyond that. I know you're someone capable of reflection and growth."

I went back to a cheerful tone as I finished speaking. That was when I realized Ayase was no longer walking next to me.

I turned around and saw her frozen in place, three steps behind me.

"Ayase?"

She was hanging her head, which worried me a little.

"Asamura, you…"

This time, her voice was almost too soft to hear in the rain.

"You *understand me too well*."

Did she really say that?

She looked up, set her gaze straight ahead, and briskly walked past me. Then she made her way through the gate before disappearing behind a screen of rain and other people.

"What's up, Asamura?"

I stood there under my umbrella, looking dazed, until Maru slapped me on the shoulder. I noticed the area he'd slapped felt awfully cold, then realized that I hadn't been holding my umbrella straight and my shoulder had gotten wet.

The image of Ayase from behind, just before she vanished into the crowd, was burned into my memory.

When the bell rang, signaling the end of the day, it still hadn't stopped raining.

It was Thursday, and I had to work. I would need to return home first and then head to the bookstore. Traveling back and forth in the rain sounded like a real hassle. It probably would have been easier to bring my work uniform and go straight there after school.

Walking down the hall, I looked through the window. The drizzle seemed to blur the scene outside.

It wasn't that I didn't like the rainy season. On the contrary, it made the green leaves more vivid, and the smell of it reminded me that summer was on its way.

That said, I always tried to carry as little as possible whenever it rained, and because I was responsible for cleaning my uniform if it got dirty, I kept it at home instead of leaving it at work.

I walked toward the shoe lockers at the front of the school, checking left and right without thinking. When I realized what I was doing, I shook my head. Honestly, there was no way she would be out there staring at the rain again. She had her umbrella when we walked to school that morning.

"She must have gone home by now."

I opened the big men's umbrella in my hand. Its dark circle obscured a large part of the scene in front of me, and for a moment, I couldn't see a thing. Then I leaned it against my shoulder and stepped out.

I'd brought Dad's plain umbrella instead of my folding one partly because it'd been raining since morning, but also in case someone had spotted Ayase with mine the day before.

Maybe I didn't need to be so careful about things like that. We were siblings, after all. She was my stepsister—my little sister—though that had been true for less than a week at this point. And though I believed I was gradually coming to understand her, I kept wondering what she'd meant that morning.

The sound of the rain against the top of my umbrella was too loud and kept distracting me from my thoughts.

I reached our apartment building and stepped into our home. The sound of raindrops echoing in my ears stopped as soon as I shut the thick door behind me.

I closed my umbrella, set it on a stand, and exhaled. Then I removed my shoes, which had grown wet and heavy. I felt cold, but there was no time for a bath. I had to get moving.

I went to my room, passing Ayase's on the way. I didn't mean to peek, but the door was open a crack, and I caught a glimpse of the interior. Colorful underwear and other clothes had been hung inside, right where anyone could see them.

Well, of course. It *was* raining.

I was the type who would throw anything I washed in the dryer, but I was aware that some people hung-dry certain items so they wouldn't be damaged.

Still.

Who would have thought the day would come when I would see a full lineup of women's clothes and underwear in my home? Ugh, but I shouldn't be staring, should I?

If her wet clothes were hung out to dry, Ayase must be home already. If she saw me looking at them, it wouldn't just be awkward—I'd be in big trouble.

"Asamura? I didn't know you were home."

"Eep!"

I heard a voice from behind me, and I immediately straightened up. I pivoted so fast, I could swear the air made a sound as my body cut through it.

"What's the matter?" Ayase asked.

"Oh, nothing. Nothing at all."

"No? Well okay, then," she said, still staring at me suspiciously.

"I, uh, have to work today."

I waved at her casually and headed for my room. I could feel her gaze on my back but lacked the courage to turn around. I felt like I'd just stolen a pair of panties.

All I did was see her clothes accidentally. I'd done nothing wrong. Besides, Ayase herself had said that underwear was no different from a handkerchief after it was washed. Nevertheless, I felt guilty.

I shoved my work uniform into my bag, ran out the door, and headed for the bookstore. But even the pounding of the rain couldn't cover the sound of my beating heart.

I poured myself into my work.

I wanted to erase the memories of a little while ago from my mind—in particular, my memory of a certain piece of blue cloth.

I changed into my uniform, put my name tag on my shirt, and tried to lose myself in my job.

I was currently sorting through the inventory, removing books that had sat on the shelf for a certain period of time without selling. This was something we had to do to make space for new arrivals.

The next day was a Friday; our wholesaler didn't usually deliver on weekends, so every book launched on Saturday and Sunday would arrive then.

That meant we needed more shelf space.

Regardless of how accurately corporate estimated the sales for each store, it was never perfect. You simply couldn't predict what would catch people's interest or what might motivate them, and there was a strong element of chance. Uncertainty and chaos were constantly present in the mix. We never sold every book we stocked, and we probably never would. There were always books that got left behind.

*Oh, this one didn't sell...*

I picked up a certain book while checking over the light novel section. I'd noticed it when I first stocked it on the shelf. The author had probably wanted to avoid making another forgettable harem-style romcom, but I think he overdid it, cramming the faces of forty-eight girls right on the cover. It was a little *too* original.

Books that authors and publishers thought would sell were not always the same ones that sold. Unfortunately, many customers were conservative in their tastes.

I separated the book from my stack of outgoing stock and continued sorting through the shelf.

"Picking out books for yourself again?"

I turned and saw Yomiuri standing behind me.

"If no one buys it," I said, "we'll just have to return it to the wholesaler, so I thought I could help boost our numbers a little...but I wonder why we stocked this book in the first place."

Chain bookstores usually had a grasp of what books would sell based on past performance. Sure, there were fluctuations, but this book seemed unusually niche. Or at least I thought so. I supposed I liked it, though.

"It must be because people buy unique and original books like that every month!"

"You think so?"

Yomiuri stared at me and grinned.

*Huh?* Was she implying that I was one such customer?

"Heh-heh. Anyway, I noticed that you've been working hard today."

"Please don't make it sound unusual. I always work hard."

"You do?"

"Do you think I'm acting strange?"

"Seeing you so immersed in your work, I wondered if something bad might have happened to you."

"You sound like an all-seeing hermit sage."

"That's got a nice ring to it. If I was a hermit sage, I wouldn't have to worry about all the goings-on down here in the mortal realm. *Haah.*"

Her sigh made me wonder what goings-on she was referring to.

"What about you?" I asked. "Did something happen to you?"

"You want to know?"

"Sure, if there's any reason I should know."

"Good answer! That's what I love about you!"

"As I keep saying, remarks like that will lead to misunderstandings."

She grinned devilishly when she spoke—proof she had a wicked personality.

"I'm fine for now," she said. "I feel better already, knowing I have a young protégé who pays attention to me."

"Oh, really?"

"Yeah. So…"

"Yes?"

"…make sure you pay attention to your cute little sister, too."

"Wh-what?!"

"Get her something sweet on your way home if you upset her."

"I—I haven't upset her."

Yet.

"Then what have you done?"

"I haven't done anything to her."

"Then maybe you did something *alone*?"

"Don't try to slip in that kinda innuendo all casual-like. I'd appreciate it if you'd stop making dirty jokes…"

"Ah-ha-ha. Well, you can't just get rid of your feelings once they're there, you know. You have to let it out little by little, or it'll build up until you explode."

Ugh. I couldn't think of a thing to say back to that. Yomiuri waved and returned to work before I could reply, leaving only a memory of her grinning face.

"She really is something else…"

Muttering to myself, I turned my attention back to the shelf behind me and resumed my work.

A bookstore clerk must always remain flexible, even while engaging in simple tasks. As long as we wore our work uniform, customer calls for help continued ceaselessly.

The most common question was where a certain book was located. These were often inquiries a search tool couldn't help with. The customer might not know the author's or publisher's name, and they might have only a vague idea of the title and genre. Someone might expect me to find a book based only on the fact that it was a series where murders occurred. With search terms that vague, it'd be impossible to locate using a computer. Or rather, the problem was that you'd get too many hits. You needed something…a little more substantial.

Just now, a customer was looking for a story about a cat that solved cases. A cat?

When I asked Yomiuri about it, she immediately led the customer to the right section. She'd said before that she liked mysteries.

"That one's famous," she said. "I'm surprised you've never heard of it."

"Oh, really?"

Mysteries were not my forte.

"If they hadn't been certain it was a cat and not, say, a dog, I might have hesitated, though," she said.

"Don't tell me there's a dog detective story, too?"

"There is."

*Wow. Mystery authors are amazing.*

There were a variety of other things a bookstore clerk had to do: accepting reservations for new book purchases, dealing with complaints from customers who didn't get the promised freebies with a magazine, and taking care of lost children.

Between handling jobs like these, I kept myself busy sorting through the shelves. Before I realized it, I had finished my work for the day. Finally, my shift was over, so I said good-bye to Yomiuri and headed home.

By the time I left the bookstore, the rain had stopped, and I could see a round moon against the clear sky, peeking out between buildings.

The moon looked different depending on the season. It rose low in the sky during summer when the sun was high, then switched positions in winter. The summer solstice hadn't arrived yet, so it was still relatively low. As a result, the full moon seemed a little uncomfortable, squeezed between two buildings.

The air remained slightly damp, but the breeze blowing through the street felt good.

I was walking when the phone I had shoved in my pants pocket began to vibrate. I pulled it out and checked my lock screen, where I saw a one-line preview of a new text message.

It disappeared shortly, but I didn't have to swipe it to know who had sent it. It was from Ayase. It was the first message she'd ever sent me.

**You were looking, weren't you?**

It was the worst first line imaginable. I already knew what the rest would say. I nervously launched the app from the lock screen and read the message.

To summarize, this is what it said:

After seeing me act strangely in front of her door, Ayase thought about it and suspected I had been looking at the underwear she had hung up in her room. She considered underwear no different from handkerchiefs but wanted to confirm why I was looking... That was the gist of it.

I did my best to explain myself in a reply and sent it before making my way toward home and the interrogation that was no doubt waiting for me there.

When I saw the shoes lined up at our door, I felt relief wash over me. Fortunately, our parents were still out. Then I looked up, and my eyes met Ayase's where she stood imposingly, her arms crossed.

"Hi, Ayase."

"Welcome back, Asamura."

It was the same greeting as always, but for some reason, it rang coldly in my ears.

"Don't just stand there," she said.

"Oh, right..."

I had given her a basic explanation, but I wasn't sure how much of it she believed...

"Come on in," she said. "Go ahead."

"Huh? Go where?"

"Oh, are you still interested in my room?"

"I'll wait for you in mine."

It was probably better not to argue at a time like this. I went to my room, sat up straight in a kneeling position, and waited for Ayase.

"Why are you sitting on the floor?" she asked when she arrived.

"Um, no particular reason."

I couldn't bring myself to say that this position would make it easier to grovel in apology. I didn't know if she would forgive me even if I did that.

"Here," she said.

"Huh?"

I raised my head and saw her holding a mug out to me.

"Don't you like hot cocoa? I'll return it to the kitchen if you don't want it."

"Oh, uh, sure...I like it," I said as I accepted the mug.

I preferred coffee, but I was grateful for anything hot after running through the cold rain.

Wait? Was that why she was offering this to me?

I looked up at Ayase's face and saw her eyes were still filled with anger.

"So...about what you wrote."

"Oh yeah."

"You said the door was half-open, and what you saw inside captured your attention. Then you heard my voice and ran."

"Right."

"Did you think I'd suspect you were about to go in and steal something?"

"I...guess so."

"Even though I'm your stepsister?"

"Well, yeah..."

I was at a loss for words. I couldn't argue. If this were my biological mom or sister, it might still be embarrassing, but would I be worried to this extent...? Ugh, there was no use thinking like that.

Ayase and I had been siblings for only five days. As I was thinking of ways to excuse myself, for some reason, Ayase was the one who frowned.

"Sorry, that wasn't fair."

"What do you mean?"

"We're legally siblings, but expecting you to suddenly act like my brother the moment the law says so—even down to your thoughts—isn't looking at you as a human being."

"…I get what you're saying."

We, as high school students, were allowed to live together under the same roof because our family had a common understanding that Ayase and I were going to behave like siblings, at least superficially.

We were expected to act as such, and our parents trusted us to do that. We couldn't betray them, and I didn't intend to, either. I would never cause trouble for Dad and Akiko.

But that didn't mean we could do everything like real siblings who'd grown up together for sixteen years. Human thoughts weren't like a program where you only had to rewrite the coding.

It was a fact that we'd been strangers until a week ago. Ayase was saying she had a duty to understand that. She always placed great importance on being fair, after all.

"Okay, now we're even. We don't owe each other anything. How's that?" she said.

"We're even?"

"I believe you being captivated by my underwear was a reflexive reaction. I was the one who acted reflexively this morning; then you did the same, so we're even. I know you're someone capable of reflection and growth."

"That's good to hear."

"By the way."

*Hmm?*

"Does this mean my underwear was so appealing that you couldn't look away?"

"I didn't say that."

"Then you had no interest… Hmm, I see."

"…Are you teasing me by any chance?"

"Who can say? But someone needs to clear the air, right?"

"I guess so."

"So somewhere deep down, you do want to steal my underwear?"

"Ugh. I guess I'd be lying if I said I'm not interested, but I'm not going to steal anything."

"Oh, so you *are* interested."

"It'd be weird if I wasn't. But being interested and acting on it isn't the same thing."

I tried to maintain a fairly serious expression as I looked at her.

"Huh. Right. I'm sorry I teased you. Let's drop it," she said.

"I would appreciate that…"

I was honestly grateful, even amazed by her reaction.

We couldn't erase our feelings on the matter, even if it had been a misunderstanding. The fact remained that she was upset that I had looked at her underwear. But instead of getting emotional about it, she told me how she felt, keeping calm the whole time. She had truly impressive control over her anger.

I still had a long way to go if I wanted to meet her where she was.

"I'm glad, though," she said after a while.

"Huh?"

"I'm glad you didn't think the design of my underwear was odd. I would have wanted to throw them away if you'd made some weird remark about it."

"…I think I may be starting to understand you."

"Yeah?"

"A little."

Ayase smiled slightly when she heard that.

# ● JUNE 12 (FRIDAY)

Ayase had been avoiding me since the morning.

At least, I got the feeling she was. I didn't know why.

She left early, before I came to the breakfast table, without saying a word to me.

I didn't know what was going on. I remembered the way she'd smiled at me the night before. I was sure I'd gotten closer to her than ever before.

No matter how hard I thought about it, I couldn't figure it out. If it had rained, we could have gone to school together again and talked. But the weather never turns out how you want it to.

It was sunny.

Pedaling my bike, I looked up at the June sky. It was a frustrating, dazzling blue. It reminded me of the phrase *beautiful May weather*.

Incidentally, when this phrase was coined, it referred to May in the lunar calendar, which corresponds to the period between the end of May and early July in our solar calendar. So most of that beautiful May weather came around in June, not May. That placed it in the rainy season, meaning it actually referred to the sunny spells we had between rain showers.

This was all information easily found online. But I had to focus on stuff like that or I'd end up thinking about Ayase all the time.

I rode my bike along the route to school. I could see signs of last night's rain on the trees that lined the street. Water droplets that had accumulated on the leaves fell now and then, hitting my wind-chapped face.

The cold drops helped reset my sleepy brain.

Maybe she was still mad about the previous day's underwear incident.

After thinking about it for a while, I decided that probably wasn't the case. Ayase seemed like the kind of person who would tell me if she was angry.

Lost in thought, I arrived at school.

I looked up at the sky. Not a single cloud.

We had PE in second period… We'd be practicing for Sports Day again on the same tennis courts as last time. My class would double up with Ayase's.

First period was modern Japanese, but I couldn't focus and barely remembered what we did. Then it was time for second period; I made my way to the tennis court and casually looked over at the girls.

"Taaake thaaat!!"

Narasaka was in terrific condition as usual. Her hits were fantastic, and she sent the ball flying into the next court.

"Hey, Narasaka!"

"Ohhh! A home run!"

"Shut up!"

I didn't think there were home runs in tennis.

Ayase wasn't among the girls cheerfully practicing. She was standing alone in a corner, leaning against the fence again, her earphones in her ears. But this time, she wasn't looking vaguely into thin air like before. Instead, she appeared to be thinking hard about something.

Her face was turned down, and her eyes were closed. It worried me.

Narasaka walked over to my side at the end of class and whispered in my ear.

"Hey, *Big Brother.*"

Did she have to start that again at school? I was about to make a comeback when she caught me off guard.

"Has something happened to Saki?"

Her words hit like a sucker punch and left me speechless. Narasaka had also noticed that Ayase was acting differently.

"I don't know," I said.

"I see."

Seemingly puzzled and mumbling to herself, Narasaka crossed her arms and walked toward the school building. A few girls waiting to use the court glanced at me. *It's not what you're thinking, okay?*

"Hey, Asamura."

"Huh? Oh, Maru, it's you."

I turned around and saw my best friend standing behind me.

"You sound distracted," he said.

"I'm just tired from practice."

"When you aren't out of breath and don't have a single speck of dirt on your clothes?"

"You're really paying attention."

As for Maru, it appeared softball practice had been busy for him that day. He was covered with dirt.

"What are you staring at?" he asked. "Do you want my body?"

"I was just thinking it's going to be a nightmare washing those clothes."

"Huh. I wouldn't mind selling my body to you if you paid me ten thousand yen."

He was offering to sell his...body?

"Wh-what are you talking about?!"

"That's about the right amount for a day of physical labor. I've done almost everything, from fixing leaky roofs to building doghouses. I think it's fair for a one-day gig."

"...Oh, that's what you meant."

"Come on, Asamura. What were you thinking?"

Like I could say that out loud.

"Unfortunately," I said, "we don't have leaks in our roof, since we live on the third floor of an apartment building, and we have no plans to build a doghouse. We don't even have a dog."

"You don't? Too bad. I figured it was a good way to make some quick cash."

"Hey, that doesn't sound like what you told me the other day."

Didn't you need to learn about how society worked and how to run a business to make money?

"Settle down. I only meant a onetime deal. A birthday's coming up."

"Whose?"

Oh. He clammed up.

"So you want money to buy someone a birthday present. Is that it?" I asked.

"You'd better hurry, or you'll be late for your next class."

With that, he turned his back on me and walked away. So Maru had someone he wanted to give a birthday present to, did he?

In the end, I wasn't able to talk to Ayase at school, so I sent her a text message.

**You're quiet today. Has something happened?**

**No. Nothing.**

Not even one emoji—not that Ayase seemed the type to use them. But her brusque response made her feel distant.

I went straight to work on my bicycle after school.

As usual, Yomiuri kept subtly teasing me, but I managed to get through the evening and sped back home on my bike.

I opened the door to the fragrant aroma of miso soup wafting out from the kitchen and tickling my nostrils. So Ayase was already back.

"I'm home," I said and went inside.

"Welcome... Dinner's ready."

There seemed to be a subtle difference in our energy levels. Or was I reading too much into the situation?

"Are we having sashimi today?"

A blue plate with white daikon-radish garnish and thick fish slices was set on the table. It appeared to be bonito.

"Yeah. Seared bonito."

"It looks nice and fresh."

It seemed that we were having traditional Japanese food tonight. The miso soup contained potatoes sliced in half-moon shapes and seaweed scattered around them. Warm potatoes raise your body temperature—perfect for unseasonably cold weather during the rainy season. There were small bowls containing pickled cucumber slices and pickled radish, too. We didn't have big pickling containers at home, so these must have been store-bought.

Ayase brought the food to the table once I'd wiped it clean. Next, I boiled some water, then poured fresh, hot tea from the pot into cups.

"Thanks for the meal!" I said, then reached for the miso soup.

I inserted my chopsticks into my bowl, stirred the miso, and brought it to my mouth. Its aroma floated up as I pressed lightly against the contents and sipped.

"Mm. Your miso soup is really good."

"...Yeah?"

"How do I explain it? You can tell you use a good soup stock. It just tastes like miso."

"Of course it does. It's miso soup."

She sounded like she thought I was crazy.

"Not all miso soups are like that," I countered.

It wasn't as if I had never cooked in my life. But I couldn't make miso soup this good. For some reason, what I wound up with only vaguely resembled miso soup.

Long after I stopped cooking, I found out why from a book. I'd been mixing in the miso and then boiling the soup. The flavor evaporates when you do that. The flavor of miso comes from alcohol, which forms during the fermentation process. Obviously, that evaporates when boiled. Once you understand the reason, it makes perfect sense.

If I had known things like that sooner, I might have developed an interest in cooking...

"Okay, let's move on to today's main dish," I said.

"You're exaggerating."

"No, I'm not. This looks *really* good."

I placed chopped ginger on top of a fat slice of bonito, picked it up with my chopsticks, and dipped it in a small dish of soy sauce. Then I took a bite. It was chewy, and the flavor spread across my tongue. It tasted good.

"It's delicious."

Next, I added a little rice.

"This is great. Ayase, you're a good cook."

"You know…all I did was slice that fish, but thanks. It was on sale…"

"Oh, wow. You even waited for a bargain."

"I want to save money if I can."

Come to think of it, Dad and Akiko must have given her food money now that she was doing the cooking. That meant she'd have funds left over if she got things at discounted prices.

I suddenly wanted to ask her something that had been on my mind. In hindsight, that might have been the trigger.

"Why are you so interested in making money?"

Ayase stopped moving her chopsticks. They slowly hovered back and forth over the bonito, but I wasn't about to point out her bad manners. I knew she wasn't pondering what to eat. So I simply waited until she was ready to speak.

"I think I told you this before," she said, "but in order to free myself from bothersome things like people's attention and expectations, I need the ability to live independently."

"And money will give you that, huh?"

"Am I wrong?"

"Nah…I don't think you're wrong."

It was true that without money, you didn't have the freedom to do various things. But I didn't want to say that money was everything. Even I knew that was too shortsighted.

"It's tough to earn money, though." She sighed.

Her long hair fell over the white apron she was wearing on top of her school uniform as she moved. She listlessly set down her chopsticks and pulled her hair back.

"I'm still looking for that high-paying part-time job for you...," I said.

"I didn't think it would be easy."

That might be true, but the fact that she was keeping up her end of the deal and cooking for me made me uncomfortable.

"I want you to tell me if you'd like more help," I offered. "Or you could cut corners with your cooking."

"I am."

"You make sure to finish cooking breakfast in half an hour and then spend only an hour on dinner, right?"

She gasped. "You noticed."

"Sure I did."

Of course I'd noticed. Ayase was always glancing at the clock while she cooked, and I knew she wasn't using it as a food timer. She'd been hesitant to gather information on jobs because she thought it would take time away from her studies, after all.

"Anyway," she said. "I'm not interested in spending more time than I do now to prepare meals regardless of whether I have a recipe. That's cutting corners, isn't it?"

She looked at me as if to say, "I'm terrible, right?"

"I don't think so."

She seemed surprised.

"Why not?"

"Well, you improve your skills when you do a task over and over. That usually makes you more efficient, and the quality of your work may improve, too."

"...And?"

"You can still spend an hour cooking, but you may be able to do a better job...and make tastier meals. In that case, I would have to enhance the value of what I give in exchange. It's only fair."

"Oh, forget it."

"I mean it. So far, I haven't been able to provide you with anything, and I feel like it won't be a fair trade."

"That's ridiculous. That logic would apply to all the housework in the world, with the value soaring higher and higher every day of the week."

"It does. It's all the same."

I didn't just mean cooking; I was talking about washing, cleaning, sewing—everything.

People improved their skills to a certain degree in all types of jobs.

That's why salaries increase according to the number of years you're employed. That continues until the quality and quantity of your work decrease due to aging, and the same could essentially be said of housework.

"My mom has been making my meals for years," she said, "but I don't think she's ever received a single yen for any of it."

"The value of something doesn't become clear until you exchange it for something else. For example, you don't realize the value of housework until you outsource it. It becomes clear how much it's worth when you hire someone to do the same work. That's what makes it complicated."

Recently, I'd been reading books about labor and money, and I couldn't help sprinkling in complicated ideas and concepts—so much so that I'd almost fooled myself into thinking I was smart. It was all secondhand knowledge, though.

"You and I have an exchange going here. You do the cooking, and I look for a part-time job for you, right? So that's where value enters the picture. I've put a value on your cooking, and I have to provide something with equal value in exchange."

Ayase stopped talking. It looked like she was thinking.

While I couldn't back down after saying all that, there was actually an easy way to resolve the issue, though it wasn't very favorable. I was about to tell her when she spoke up.

"...Dinner's going to get cold. Let's finish eating. Oh, and I've also drawn a bath."

"O-okay."

I'd missed my chance. I quietly picked at the food in front of me with my chopsticks.

All the while, Ayase looked down without meeting my eyes. She appeared to be thinking.

I took a bath, and as usual, I drained the tub and ran fresh hot water for Ayase. Then I changed into my nightclothes and lay in bed reading a book.

It wasn't that I had no homework to do, but I was still at the stage where I didn't need to panic. There was also Saturday and Sunday. It wouldn't hurt to look at the book I'd bought...

I was going through the light novel I'd found while working. The one with beautiful girls all over the cover.

...I'd thought it was just pulp fiction, but it was quite interesting...

...Still, was this guy really trying to date every girl in his class...his... class...?

All of a sudden, the book fell on my face with a *fwap!*

"Whoa!"

I cried out, stunned. My heart was racing.

"Oh...maybe I should get some sleep."

I felt pretty tired. I glanced at the clock and saw it wasn't that late. Dad would have usually been home by now, but I hadn't heard anyone come in the door. It was Friday. Maybe someone had taken him out drinking, and he wasn't able to refuse. That said, I knew he'd do anything to make the last train home.

I heard a *click*, and the light in my room went out.

There was another *click*, and it went into night mode. I could make out the door opening a crack in the dim orange of the room as a line of white cut through the darkness. Then the door was quietly shut. Someone had slipped in. It had to be Ayase—she was the only one in the apartment besides me. If it wasn't, that would mean it was a burglar.

What did she want in my room? And why had she turned out the light?

Was she so tired that she had mistaken my room for hers?

I was about to call out to her when I swallowed my words.

"Asamura? You're awake, aren't you?"

I smelled Ayase's sweet body soap as she approached me.

I gasped, but not because she had just come out of the bathroom. I'd already seen her like that several times.

She was the last one to take a bath.

She was the last one to go to bed.

Those were her rules. Still, I inevitably saw her during those hours every once in a while. For example, one time, I had gotten up in the middle of the night, walked into the kitchen for a glass of water, and run into her wearing a nightgown... It had been stimulating for a high school guy like me, but what was happening now went way beyond that.

I heard the scraping sound of fabric. The *flap* of clothes falling on the floor. She was clearly taking off what she was wearing.

The light beyond the door was shut out completely, and my vision was limited, as if I was in the twilight. I couldn't really see the colors, but the shape of Ayase's body was firmly etched into my brain.

I could make out the curve of her narrow waist down to her round hips. Her slim arms stretching below her shoulders. If someone wore a nightgown, those things wouldn't be visible.

In other words, Ayase was clad in only her underwear. My eyes were mesmerized by the way her hips swayed with every step she took.

"Asamura. I want to talk to you."

She was only a step away from my bed when she stopped, as if hesitating.

"You want to talk...?"

My mouth was dry, and my voice was hoarse.

She took that last step toward me, placed her hands on either side of my body, and bent down. She looked into my face, and our eyes met.

"Do you think you could buy my body?"

She was so close that I could feel her breath on my skin.

I could see her face, backlit by the pale ceiling light.

"Huh...?"

For a moment, my mind went blank.

What in the world did she just say?

I couldn't see her expression because her face was turned down and shaded in the dim light. Her voice shook as she repeated the question.

"Well? Do you think you could?"

"Wh-what do you mean?"

"Exactly what I asked. I want to know if you would buy my body. If you would be willing to pay money for it."

"……"

"I know from the incident the other day that my body is, uh, able to excite you. And, um…you don't have to go all the way. I'm asking if you could use it."

"Hey, now…," I started.

"I thought about it rationally and arrived at this conclusion."

What did *rationally* mean again?

"Think about it," she said.

"Uh, okay."

With my ability to reason quickly failing, I did my best to hold on.

"We're mature high school students," she said.

"…Yeah, I guess."

"So, uh, you know. There are some things you do that you'd rather keep private, right?"

Things you do that you'd rather keep private—she must be talking about what girls and boys did after puberty, right?

I guess she was right. There was no use denying it. So okay, my answer was yes. I'm no saint. I'm a regular high school guy. It's useless to try to hide it, but I never thought I'd be talking about it with a girl my age.

"As long as we continue to live under the same roof, there may be mishaps where we run into each other on such an occasion."

"I'd rather not imagine that."

"I started thinking about it, and it's only a problem because we don't expect it. But on the other hand, if we do it together with mutual consent from the outset, there will be advantages for both of us."

"Where did you get an idea like that…?"

"You seem to think highly of my cooking…"

I was confused at this change of subject; then I finally realized she was talking about dinner.

"…That was when it came to me. I can ask you to pay for my cooking and earn money without too much trouble."

"I guess…so."

That had also crossed my mind. It was the not-so-favorable way to resolve our issue that I'd been thinking about, and it appeared that Ayase had arrived at the same conclusion.

"I can't ask for a lot…but my costs would be minimal," she said.

"Sounds like a good idea."

Then she shook her head.

"To me, it doesn't seem worth paying for. The *take* on my part is too big. But I want money, so I thought about what I could offer that would be worth cash."

"Are you saying you considered high-paying part-time jobs with little risk and came up with the idea of selling yourself to a family member?"

She nodded.

Her thoughts were running wild in the wrong direction.

"That kind of job…might be a little awkward," she admitted, "but I think you're a better choice than a stranger, and you would probably use birth control if we went all the way."

She had even considered working with strangers.

"And I didn't think I'd feel bad about taking large amounts of money from you in exchange," she continued.

Something snapped in my mind. I got up and stretched out a hand.

Ayase's shoulder twitched. I felt guilty seeing her genuine response but stuck with my iron resolve.

"Ayase, you're acting like the type of girl I hate the most."

"Huh…?!"

I don't like bad-mouthing people. No one wants to hear words that will hurt them, regardless of the reason, and it felt terrible to speak this way.

But I had to do this.

I had to stop Ayase from doing what she was doing, no matter what it took.

I thought about Dad and Akiko.

I knew how desperate Dad had been after his ex-wife betrayed him. When was the last time I'd seen him so happy? I'd been appalled witnessing him acting so lovey-dovey and head over heels in love with his new wife, but I was also relieved to see him full of joy and wanted to cheer him on.

The same went for Akiko. I didn't know what she'd been through, but she must have divorced her ex-husband because they had issues. Dad and Akiko were so content that you would never have guessed their pasts.

If Ayase did this, it would only cause our parents disappointment and sorrow. That wasn't something I could go along with.

Ayase and I had initially agreed not to expect anything from each other, and we had been trying to maintain a comfortable distance ever since. I'd expected her not to do something like this, and my emotions now were the result of that expectation. In a way, I'd betrayed our promise.

But in terms of our initial intentions, Ayase was the one who'd strayed from our agreement.

"I thought you didn't want people to accuse you of using your appearance as a weapon," I said.

I didn't know why she felt so strongly about being looked down on as a woman, but what she was doing now was playing right into the kind of stereotype she hated.

The kind of supply and demand that Ayase was talking about existed. I wasn't denying that. People tended to see those who dated for money and worked in the entertainment district as fools who wanted quick cash. But I had heard that many of them were highly educated, intelligent women.

Maybe it wasn't unusual for a rational girl like Ayase to arrive at such a conclusion. Still, this was taking the easy way out. Not to mention, it contradicted her beliefs.

Unfortunately, I had no affection for people who caused trouble for others by refusing to resolve such contradictions. I would simply ignore them if they were strangers, but I couldn't do that to Ayase as her brother and a member of her family.

I wrapped the thin summer blanket I'd been using around her so she wouldn't get cold.

"You have to prove yourself in a way that doesn't rely on being a woman. Otherwise, there's no point."

"B-but I could do this even if I were a guy. So it doesn't necessarily mean I'm using my femininity as a weapon."

Was she saying she would have done the same thing if she were my stepbrother?

For a minute, I imagined Ayase with a boy's figure wearing flimsy clothes and looking at me with a saucy expression. I got the feeling that could have led to some real mistakes as well and quickly erased the delusion from my mind.

"No quibbling," I said firmly.

"R-right. Sorry."

She dropped her head, perhaps noting the ice in my voice. Seeing this made me anxious and frustrated. I had gotten to know her and learned that she was nothing like the rumors, and yet here she was, about to turn into the girl everyone believed her to be. I had just discovered a fine line existed, and she could go either way.

*Geez.*

I was glad I was her first attempt...

"It's okay as long as you've understood," I said. "And, uh, about your, um... You don't have to provide any compensation; I'm okay with paying for food. But there's one problem."

That was why I didn't think it was a favorable solution.

"A problem...?"

She looked a little doubtful.

"Our household income won't increase if we're just trading money around within the family."

"...What do you mean?"

"Our parents are busy, and it's tough for them to find the time to go grocery shopping. That's why they give us money each month in addition to our allowance, so we can buy the household items we need right away."

"Y-yeah."

"And I have a part-time job, too, so I can pay for the food you make. But take a moment to think. Say I got sick and couldn't work or get paid. Your income would dry up. But would you stop cooking?"

"As long as you're depending on family members for income, you can't be sure if you'll be able to receive fair compensation for your labor."

"You're right. I hadn't thought of it that way."

"Of course, there's an advantage to being paid by family. You aren't likely to be ripped off. When you work outside the home, you have to be careful to avoid people underpaying you. But even if your wages aren't that high, I think it's better to seek money from outside."

Ayase closed her mouth. She must be thinking about what I'd said.

"That's all the advice from me. I'll keep looking for a part-time job for you with good compensation, but we can't have any more of this."

"Okay... Sorry."

"Mm." I accepted her apology. I wasn't the kind to lecture someone for hours. "But maybe we need to talk a little more."

"Huh?"

"I honestly didn't think you were the type who would do something like this."

"Well, I didn't, either."

"I think this happened because I didn't have a firm grasp of who you were. So I'd like to get to know you a little better."

"...Yeah. I'm not fond of talking about my past, but I kinda caused you a lot of trouble."

Ayase closed her eyes for a minute, took a deep breath, and began speaking quietly about a memory from when she was a little girl.

She said her dad had been a talented entrepreneur.

But he stopped trusting people after his colleagues betrayed him and stole his company. He developed an inferiority complex and grew distant from his wife and daughter.

"An inferiority complex?" I asked.

"Thinking about it now, maybe he was jealous. Mom often said a high school graduate like her could only make a living working in bars, but when you speak with her coworkers, you can tell she's super popular."

"Your mom's a good talker. And she's bright and cheerful."

"Yeah...I think my dad was nice when I was little, but he changed after losing his business."

He eventually stopped coming home, found another woman, and began to hang around her all the time. He no longer brought any money home, leaving Akiko to support Ayase alone. She was able to, but that only made her husband hate her even more.

Forced to acknowledge his wife's capabilities, he grew even more miserable and started insulting her job and saying he thought she was cheating on him.

"But none of that gave him the right to put her through hell," Ayase said.

So that was why Ayase felt the way she did about those stereotypes...

"Of course not," I agreed, a little more firmly than I'd intended. I meant it.

Ayase looked up and stared at me again.

"Asamura?"

"Oh, um, sorry. This reminds me of what happened to Dad."

"Really?"

"Yeah. He practically had a pathological fear of women for a little while.

That's why I was surprised when he got remarried. Akiko must have finally cured him."

"Your dad had a fear of women?"

"Yeah."

"I see…"

I heard her ask, "You too?" softly but pretended I didn't.

"So that's why you keep a subtle distance from my mom…," Ayase muttered. I guess she'd noticed me having a hard time figuring out how to act around Akiko. "I think we're similar kinds of people," Ayase said.

"Maybe we are."

"Including our faults."

I laughed. There was no denying that.

"So anyway," I said, "I think we'll be able to get along, our faults included. I mean, as siblings."

"As…siblings?"

"Yeah."

A faint smile appeared on Ayase's face, and the tension seemed to drain out of her as if she had just put down a great weight.

"Sounds good to me, Asamura."

"Great. Oh, and while we're at it, you can call me *Big Brother* whenever you want."

"I don't think so."

"Awww…"

*Too bad.* Oh well, I didn't have to rush it. We were going to be siblings for a long time.

"Asamura, I don't intend to go any further, okay?"

She removed the blanket wrapped around her body, folded it, and placed it on my bed.

Then she moved her face close to mine.

"I mean that."

Her lips, which had turned rosy from her bath, propelled those words right into my face.

*Okay, already.*
*Whatever.*
My days with my pretty, somewhat-worrying stepsister had only just begun.

# ● JUNE 13 (SATURDAY)

A white tablecloth covered the dining table.

The morning light made the silver decorative patterns on the plates shine. Fried eggs, cooked in beautiful circles like full moons, were placed neatly at the center of the plates—one for Dad and one for Ayase.

"Hey, move your hand a minute," Ayase said, and I quickly stopped wiping the table and got out of the way.

"This one's yours," she said, placing another plate on the table. Omelets, lined up elegantly like hot rolled towels, sat on a blue plate. When I touched them with my chopsticks, they easily parted into bite-size slices.

"Are these *dashimaki tamago*?"

"You looked like you wanted them, and it's Saturday, so I have plenty of time. I can make them every once in a while. But I'm not sure how good they are, so don't get your hopes up," she said, slightly shy.

"Thanks."

"Did Saki make that?" Dad asked. "Wow, lucky you. Hey, Yuuta, how about sharing some with me?"

"Oh, it's nothing special," Ayase responded modestly.

"Aw, come on, it looks great. I bet it's delicious. Don't you agree, Yuuta?"

Dad looked so longingly at his stepdaughter's home-cooked eggs that I gave him a few pieces. It was like he'd forgotten that she'd made the fried eggs on his plate, too.

"Wow…everyone's up early."

I turned around at the sound of an unfamiliar voice behind me.

It was Akiko, wearing only a gown over her nightwear and rubbing her eyes like she was still sleepy.

Her hair was flying in different directions like it hadn't been brushed yet. To me, she looked a little more sexy than she did relaxed.

"What time is…it?"

She glanced at the clock and gasped.

"You're kidding…"

We were having breakfast an hour later than usual, since it was Saturday. Dad didn't have to go to work, and Ayase and I wouldn't be going to school. It was also out of consideration for Akiko, who tended to come home late and wasn't getting enough sleep.

"Go back to bed, Akiko. You were out working late again last night, weren't you?"

"It's okay, Taichi. Saki, I'm sorry you've had to do everything."

"That's okay. Hey, Mom…your outfit's a little too provocative for Asamura, and it isn't good for Dad, either."

"Huh…?!"

Akiko looked at herself and shrieked, then ran back to her bedroom.

"Oh, Akiko! Wait, I want to talk to you," Dad said, rushing after her.

"Oh boy," I said.

"Huh. It looks like her fake front's wearing off," Ayase observed.

"Yeah?"

"I've got to give her credit. It lasted a whole week."

I wasn't sure if it was okay for me to agree with that.

"To preserve her honor," Ayase continued, "I'll tell you that she's only like that when she's just gotten out of bed."

Ah. Well, I wasn't much of a morning person myself.

"I guess the blackout curtains worked," I said.

"Yeah, maybe."

The new curtains had arrived the previous day.

Besides blocking the light, they also blocked heat and sound. So the room would be cool in summer and warm in winter. Dad said it was a small price to pay if that was all it took to help Akiko sleep and stay healthy.

There was a *ping*, and Ayase went to the toaster oven. She pulled out two slices of bread and placed them on a plate.

"Tell me if you want more."

"No, that's fine."

So we were having toast this morning instead of rice. She put a couple more slices in the toaster for Dad and reset the timer. They should be ready by the time he got back to the table.

"I know toast doesn't go well with Japanese-style eggs," she said.

"It's fine."

What I meant by that was, "Thanks for going to the trouble of making them."

She had also made salad and a consommé soup. It was plenty for breakfast. I was sad we didn't have any miso soup, but I figured she had spent the time it would have taken to make it to cook the eggs.

I folded my hands together and said my thanks, then picked up my chopsticks and reached for a bite of egg.

"Mm, this is great!"

"You exaggerate."

"No, I mean it. Akiko's were good, but these are just as tasty."

"Yeah?"

"Yeah."

"Well, I'll make it for you again."

"Only if you have the time."

"Only if I have the time."

We said the same thing simultaneously and both clammed up. After that, we ate in silence for a while.

What was taking Dad so long? We were going to finish eating before he got back.

"So it's already been a week," I said.

"What's already been a week?"

"We talked about it earlier. You and Akiko moved in on Sunday, and it'll be a week tomorrow."

"So? You want to celebrate or something?"

"Huh…maybe that's not a bad idea."

"Are you serious?"

She looked at me like I was out of my mind, which made me laugh.

"I think Dad will want to celebrate when he realizes it's been a week."

"Uh…"

"Dad has always liked doing that kind of thing. But maybe it's better to give him and Akiko time to themselves."

They didn't have a wedding or go on a honeymoon, saying they'd both done all that before.

"Oh, that's a good point," said Ayase.

"Right?"

Just then, Dad and Akiko walked back into the dining area.

"Hey, kids," said Dad. "You two look like you're enjoying yourselves. What are you talking about?"

"Nothing," I quickly replied.

I'd tell Dad later to take Akiko to dinner or something.

His toast was ready, and Ayase put the bread on a plate and brought it to the table.

"Saki, I—," said Akiko.

"I know, one slice for you."

She put two thin slices of bread in the toaster and adjusted the timer.

The other slice must be for herself. She liked giving more when it came to give-and-take, and she'd prepared her portion last. She was consistent.

"One slice for you, too?" she asked me.

"I can't eat that much in the morning."

"I'll remember that."

"Thanks."

It was important to make things clear between us.

"The two of you are getting along well," Akiko said.

"Just like siblings," Dad remarked.

"It's wonderful."

Dad and Akiko smiled.

I was glad they saw it that way, though we'd almost blown it the previous night.

By the time we finished breakfast, strong sunlight was pouring in through the window. The white clouds in the sky were clear and distinct, reminding me that summer was almost here. Temperatures were rising. It wasn't so hot that we needed to turn on the air conditioner, so I opened the windows.

It was a sunny break in the middle of the rainy season.

The breeze blowing in brought our new family a whiff of the fresh foliage outside.

# ● EPILOGUE
# SAKI AYASE'S DIARY

## June 7 (Sunday)

I'm honestly relieved.
I knew when we first met that he wasn't a bad person.
I also knew he was considerate.
He's the kind of guy who will draw a new bath for me after he finishes his own.

I didn't expect him to also attend Suisei.

## June 8 (Monday)

Asamura approached me at school.

He's less emotional than I'd imagined.
I'm a little upset that he believed that rumor about me, but maybe it was inevitable. I know how other people see me.
But he was angry.
And he recognized that I was angry.
He may be the first person I've met who bothered to figure out how both of us felt and tried to reach a compromise.

## June 9 (Tuesday)

Note: Asamura likes soy sauce on his fried eggs.

Starting today, I'm handling the cooking.

It's the least I can do, since Asamura's helping me look for a part-time job with good pay.

He was apologetic and said he couldn't find one, but I didn't think it would be easy.

Cleverly relying on others, huh?

If only...I could do that.

## June 10 (Wednesday)

God, I'm so embarrassed.

I didn't think he'd hear that.

I don't want people to see me making an effort. It isn't cool.

Maaya came over to visit me in my new home. As usual, she was a noisy pain in the neck.

The three of us played a game and laughed a lot. When was the last time I laughed so much? Asamura and I also exchanged contact info.

It's just like him to have a landscape photo as his icon.

Hey, Asamura, thanks for the umbrella.

## June 11 (Thursday)

From now on, I'll be careful and make sure to close the door when I hang-dry my underwear. Yep, that's what I'll do.

Underwear is nothing more than pieces of fabric, but to think that Asamura was so captivated by them. Geez...

Fortunately, he didn't seem like he was ready to turn criminal and steal a pair.

Still...

He said he wouldn't and that having a desire and acting on it were different. I couldn't agree more.

I've noticed that I agree with all his opinions. That must be why I feel so comfortable around him.

Asamura is dangerous.

He understands me too well.

## June 12 (Friday)

Asamura chewed me out for the first time.

One thing led to another, and I told Asamura about *him* when I didn't even want to think about him. Asamura seems to have a similar past, though I didn't get around to asking him about it.

We talked a lot, but there was something I couldn't tell him.

I was so scared of owing him that I even tried to sell my body to him.

## June 13 (Saturday)

Asamura and I had dinner alone.

That was because we managed to get Mom and Dad to go out together.

Asamura suggested it. He's truly considerate.

And that's exactly why I can't call him my older brother.

If I do, I know I'll start wanting to rely on him endlessly.

I can't let that happen. Ever.

Sorry, Asamura.

But Asamura—every time I call his name, I'm filled with this feeling, and it isn't the kind of emotion you have for an older brother.

I've never felt this way before and don't know how to describe it.

My mind's fuzzy, and I'm always thinking of him.

I'm having trouble sleeping, and it doesn't help to cover my head with a blanket.

I have to play some relaxing music on my phone and slowly soothe my brain, or the tension in my body won't go away. I can't believe I can't sleep without relying on the power of music. And when I'm trying so hard to become independent. It's pathetic.

...What *is* this? Seriously.

## AFTERWORD FROM GHOST MIKAWA

Thank you for picking up a copy of *Days with My Stepsister*. I'm Ghost Mikawa, author of the original YouTube videos and this novel edition. While my job is to write novels like this and deliver them to readers, I tried to go a step further this time and create a work that would complement my readers' daily lives. Rather than writing something dramatic and filled with extreme events, I stayed faithful to my vow to show the everyday lives of Yuuta Asamura and Saki Ayase with care, depicting the gradual changes that occur. I will periodically post content on my YouTube channel and work on narrative videos and various other projects, too. I hope it will help you feel closer to the characters.

I extend my gratitude to Hiten, our illustrator; Yuki Nakashima, who plays Saki Ayase; Kouhei Amasaki, who voices Yuuta Asamura; Ayu Suzuki, who plays Maaya Narasaka; Daiki Hamano, who plays Tomokazu Maru; the video director, Yuusuke Ochiai; and the advertisers and staff handling the YouTube version. With your help, we have been able to come this far. Many thanks to every one of you!

And to my readers and fans of the videos, I hope you will continue to enjoy *Days with My Stepsister* for a long time to come.

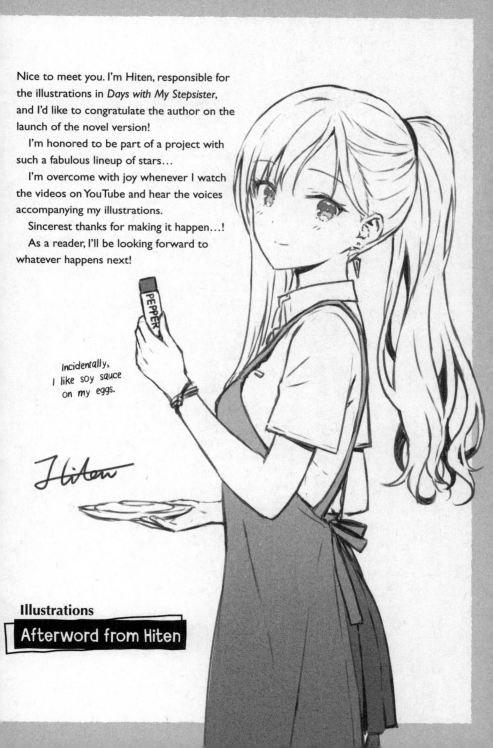

Nice to meet you. I'm Hiten, responsible for the illustrations in *Days with My Stepsister*, and I'd like to congratulate the author on the launch of the novel version!

I'm honored to be part of a project with such a fabulous lineup of stars…

I'm overcome with joy whenever I watch the videos on YouTube and hear the voices accompanying my illustrations.

Sincerest thanks for making it happen…!

As a reader, I'll be looking forward to whatever happens next!

PEPPER

Incidentally, I like soy sauce on my eggs.

*Hiten*

**Illustrations**
**Afterword from Hiten**

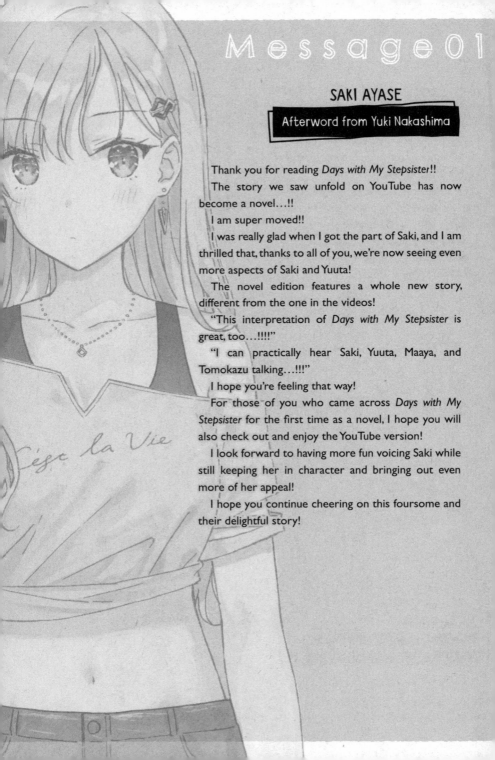

# Message01

## SAKI AYASE

### Afterword from Yuki Nakashima

Thank you for reading *Days with My Stepsister*!!

The story we saw unfold on YouTube has now become a novel…!!

I am super moved!!

I was really glad when I got the part of Saki, and I am thrilled that, thanks to all of you, we're now seeing even more aspects of Saki and Yuuta!

The novel edition features a whole new story, different from the one in the videos!

"This interpretation of *Days with My Stepsister* is great, too…!!!!"

"I can practically hear Saki, Yuuta, Maaya, and Tomokazu talking…!!!"

I hope you're feeling that way!

For those of you who came across *Days with My Stepsister* for the first time as a novel, I hope you will also check out and enjoy the YouTube version!

I look forward to having more fun voicing Saki while still keeping her in character and bringing out even more of her appeal!

I hope you continue cheering on this foursome and their delightful story!

# Message02

Thank you for reading *Days with My Stepsister* to the very end!!

Not that I wrote the story or anything. Maybe that was out of line... Ha-ha, sorry.

As the person behind Yuuta's voice since this story's beginning as a YouTube video series, I am so happy that fans can now read it as a novel, too.

I haven't read the novel yet as I write this, and I can't wait to do so!!

I have always enjoyed reading the lines spoken by novel and game characters aloud, but it's surreal knowing I'm the official voice for Yuuta!

Hooray!! I'm feeling a little giddy just thinking about it. It's been a whole year!! That's how happy I am.

To fans of the YouTube series, I'm always ecstatic to play the role of Yuuta, and I look forward to your continued support!!

Every like, channel subscription, and comment makes me super happy. ☆

I hope to see more from all you fans!!

And now, allow me to tell you about a dream I have!!

I would be beyond thrilled if I could someday play Yuuta from the novel version!!

And what's more, I would be over the moon to see the characters in motion in an anime!!

Sorry, that was two dreams.

Lastly, *Days with My Stepsister* always gets its energy from the fans who support it!!

Thank you all from the bottom of my heart!

Let's continue enjoying the story together!!

# Message03

### MAAYA NARASAKA

**Afterword from Ayu Suzuki**

I know this is abrupt, but…!

It's tough to make people happy, isn't it?! (That was abrupt!)

Maaya Narasaka, the girl I voice, is amazing; she always brightens the mood of those around her!

I truly respect her!!

I still remember my first recording as Maaya. I was moved when our staff told me that Maaya's role was to bring people joy… What a precious role…!

I'm proud to be her voice.

But Maaya isn't alone. Every character in *Days with My Stepsister* works hard for others…!

That's what I think, anyway, and I genuinely respect them all…

This is a story full of human goodness, and apart from voicing Maaya, I'm also another fan looking forward to what happens next!

I hope you'll join me on this lovely journey, and we can find out together!!

Yaaay! ☆

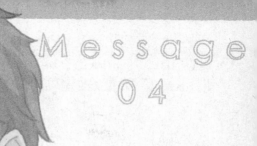

## TOMOKAZU MARU

### Afterword from Daiki Hamano

Thank you for purchasing a copy of Tomokazu Maru's first photo collection, *Tomokazu in Taiwan*.

It's thanks to you fans out there that I've...

Huh? ...That's not what you bought?

What do you mean, there are no plans to publish a photo album...?

Then what is this afterword for?

Huh?! *Days with My Stepsister* has become a novel?!

That's amazing!!! Congratulations!

I'm very excited to discover where the characters will go, now that they've traveled beyond the boundaries of YouTube. I can't wait to see how they grow.

I intend to read the book from cover to cover and deepen my understanding of the characters so I can improve my voice acting!

I hope you'll keep rooting for us on the YouTube channel, too!

Although they still haven't gotten used to living in the same home, Saki and Yuuta have managed to maintain a comfortable distance.

How will Saki's and Yuuta's lives gradually shift...

But one day, a school exam brings about a change in Saki.

*DAYS WITH MY STEPSISTER,* VOL. 2

She's been studying so hard that she looks ready to collapse, and Yuuta, worried about her, decides to do what he can to support her. He considers various ways to help, like improving her study environment and searching for music to help her focus.

...in the next installment of this true-to-life romance between siblings?

But around that same time, Shiori Yomiuri, the beautiful college student who works with Yuuta, asks him out on a date.

When Saki hears about that, she can't help a *certain feeling* bubbling up in her chest…

ON SALE IN EARLY 2024!

# STEPSISTER

## TO OUR YOUTUBE CHANNEL!

https://www.youtube.com/channel/
UCOQyW7GmCyTKwjCJEaTBWRw